CASTED

A RUNECASTER NOVEL

Written By: Izzy Clarke

Edited By: Matt Levine

TO: CJ

- Izzy
Clarke

THANK YOU!

Thank you to all the kind people who backed me on Kickstarter and made this book possible. I would like to provide a special shout out to:

Nancy Clarke
Isabel and Pat Stevens
Fred and Ann Clarke
Linda and Pat Clarke
Jeremy and Denise Lapon
Callie and John Turk
Matt and Laurice Levine

I would like to give an extra special thank you to Matt Levine for doing such a great job editing this book, and teaching me so much about writing. Your kindness, time, and effort is what made this book a reality.

Chapter 1 - A New Beginning

"Emma, what am I going to do with you? You have to be at work in five minutes, and you haven't finished breakfast." My Aunt Twila came down the stairs saying this to me. She had taken care of me ever since my parents had died in a car crash when I was eight. I was surprised that I was related to her, as she was rather pretty; whereas my brown curls always frizzed and stuck up in the wrong places, I had too many freckles, and my nose always seemed a little too big for my face. My aunt had the most beautiful face. I always wondered if she had beautiful hair too, but she always covered it up with a turban that came down over her forehead. I always wondered why she wore it, but when I asked, she would say it was for personal reasons.

"Emma, stop daydreaming, and go to work!" my aunt said. Aunt Twila also had piercing green eyes that could make a starving wolf back away from a steak with one look.

"Sorry," I replied. I grabbed my bag and headed toward the door. "Bye, Aunt Twila!" I yelled as I headed out. I hopped in my car and started driving. Aunt Twila had given me the car for my sixteenth birthday. It was a red, four-passenger Ford. It was small, but I didn't want a big car.

I pulled into my usual spot at work. The space had once said *Employee* but now only said *EMP*. The restaurant was pretty popular, even though it wasn't in a big town. Our town was just a little town out in the country of New York state. It was one of those towns where everyone on your block was like family. The sign above the door had the name of the restaurant painted onto a carved slab of wood: *Titully's*. I walked into the restaurant with my head down in an attempt to keep my boss from noticing me and yelling at me for being late.

"You're late! A customer almost left, they were waiting so long!" he yelled at me.

"I'm not your only waitress, you know," I muttered.

"What did you say?" he demanded. "Now, let's be clear about something. I'm your boss, and I can fire you anytime I want!" I just nodded.

I was running so late today, I hadn't had time to change. So, I had just thrown my clothes in my bag. I grabbed my clothes out of my bag and headed to the bathroom to change into my uniform. I was walking down the hallway to the bathroom when I glanced out the window at the parking lot and saw something glowing on the ground. What was it? Uh-oh, it looked like a phone. I would want somebody to pick it up if it were mine. I opened the nearest door and ran out to grab the phone. When I got to it, I stared. It wasn't...it couldn't be. There was no such thing as magic!

Chapter 2 – A New Introduction

I stared and stared. It was no phone—it was the oddest object I'd ever seen. It was a rock with a symbol carved in it, and the symbol was glowing like fire. Somebody must've been pulling a prank on me. It was probably plastic and from a Halloween store.

"Ha, ha, ha, very funny," I said in case the prankster was waiting nearby. The customers in the parking lot looked at me funny. Okay, nobody was pranking me. Somebody must've dropped it, or maybe it had fallen out of a car. I mean, that was the only reasonable explanation. I picked it up. It was hard as stone; in fact, it *was* stone. I had seen props like this before. It was probably just carved out with a light inside, but something about the light seemed like it wasn't artificial. It seemed like there was actual fire glowing through the surface of the stone. I stuck it in my pocket and headed back to the bathroom to change.

I leaned over the wait station. Our restaurant was very popular somehow, for breakfast, lunch, and dinner. It was very busy that day, so I was very tired even though I had only been working for an hour.

Three more people walked in. I straightened up and brushed my skirt off. Without even looking at them, their presence sent chills through me. I looked up; it was one woman and two men. Both of the men wore long black trench coats with black pants and black boots. The lady wore the same pants and boots, but instead of a trench coat, she wore a black cloak. My heart almost stopped when I saw their horrifying tattoo; it was patterned as a knife going straight down the middle of their faces. What should I do? Should I ask them about the tattoo? Run? Ask them if they'd like to dine? Were they gang members?

"How many people will be dining today?" I stuttered.

"Three," the lady said.

"Right this way." I guided them toward a table as far away from the other customers as possible. I didn't want any of them to leave because of this group. They sat down, and as I was walking back to the wait station, I glanced behind me. One of the men had pulled out a rock like the one I had found earlier, except this one was black. I stopped just as he rubbed one of his hands over it. A fireball shot straight at me! I ducked, and everybody screamed.

Chapter 3 - Discovered

Another fireball came right after the first. I climbed under a table and covered my head and neck. As soon as the next one came, I ran toward the exit. The mysterious people didn't seem to care about the people being evacuated by my manager. They just cared about hitting me with one of those horrible fireballs. Another one came flying at me. It missed, but as I dodged, I fell and hit my head on the tile floor of the kitchen. I rubbed my head and jumped up—a fireball hit the place where I was sitting seconds before.

I ran to the exit again, this time hoping to be more successful. Another fireball shot at me. I ducked, but my forehead banged against a piece of glass. Pain shot through my head. "Ahh," I whimpered. I slammed into the back door, but it didn't open. It must've locked when I came back in from picking up the rock.

The rock—that was it! Their rock was exactly like the one I found!

I grabbed the rock out of my pocket. I didn't know how to make fireballs, but throwing it at them was worth a shot. I tossed the rock as hard as I could. The last thing I remembered was a big explosion, and then everything blacked out.

A lady in a white uniform hovered over me, pressing a cool cloth onto my forehead. "Wha...what happened?" I stuttered. I stared at the giant room I was lying in. I knew I was in a hospital, but it didn't look like the hospital in my town. I had once fallen from a tree and broke my arm, and Aunt Twila had rushed me to the hospital. I clearly remembered the hospital—I was there for a whole day getting x-rays—and this room was not part of it.

"I'll explain later. Just rest. You went through a lot," the lady in white replied in a soothing voice. I was hesitant to not ask questions, but I was too tired to do anything else, so I let myself drift into a deep sleep.

When I awoke, the lady was gone. A man had replaced her. He wore only black leather, and his boots were caked in mud as if he had stepped in a big bowl of chocolate.

"Ah, Emma, you have awakened." The man spoke in a deep and calm voice.

"Where am I?" I asked.

"You're at Ebonhaunt's hospital," he answered.

"How did I get here?" I asked. Suddenly, I remembered the fireballs. "There were these men and a woman, and they were shooting fireballs with this rock. And they kept trying to hit me, but I threw one of the rocks at them, and there was an explosion," I blurted, confused about what had happened. "Who are you? Are you one of them?" I asked the man.

"My name's Colonel James. Those people in the restaurant—I am not one of them," he answered.

"How…how did you know my name?" I asked.

He pointed to the medical chart at the end of my bed. "Well, Emma, what I am about to tell you I must tell you quickly. And I understand if it is hard to believe. According to your blood test, you are the Deliverer," he told me.

"I'm sorry, the *what*?" I asked, rubbing my head. I must've hit it pretty hard. I didn't think I was hearing things right.

"The Deliverer. Surely, you've heard about the Deliverer, the most powerful rune caster in the world!" Colonel James replied.

"Um, rune caster? I'm sorry, I don't think I'm hearing correctly. Maybe I should go back to bed," I said.

"No, you're hearing everything fine," the Colonel said. "I can't believe you've never heard of rune casting. Surely... Ah, your parents didn't tell you? After all, you are a rune caster."

"No, they didn't, because that isn't a real thing, and my parents died in a car crash when I was eight years old anyway," I answered.

"Well, I'm sorry to hear that," he said.

"It's okay."

"You come from a species of humans that has the ability to cast spells using runes," the Colonel tried to explain.

"Um, there's no such things as wizards," I insisted. "I mean, that would be crazy. I'm sorry, you seem nice and everything, but I have to get some rest."

"You're exactly right, there's no such things as wizards, but there *are* rune casters. This must be a lot to take in. Trust me, I am here to help you. Just watch."

Colonel James pulled a rock like the one I had found earlier out of his pocket. He pressed it into his palm, and the lamp next to my bed began to float.

"This is crazy!" I said. "No, you're not real! I'm just dreaming, and when I go to sleep, none of this will have ever happened." The words were comforting, but something told me that they weren't true.

"Just hear me out. Emma, what's your last name?"

"Emma Westley," I said.

"Hmm, just out of curiosity, what are your parents' first names?" he asked, looking interested.

"Ben and Maria, but they died in a car crash when I was eight."

"You mean Ben Herald Westley and Maria Haley Westley?" he said. "And your aunt is Twila. Emma, your parents are alive."

I started to talk without processing the information. "If you can bring them here right now, I'll believe every word you've said."

"Yes, I'll go get them," he replied. He went to the phone and picked it up. "Ben and Maria Westley, please report to the Medical Sector, room 2331, immediately." I couldn't believe it. My real parents—they might be alive! I had so many questions that needed to be answered. What if my parents didn't want me—was that why they left me? I looked up to see a man and a woman walking through the door. The woman had dark brown hair like my hair, and the man had eyes that were the same exact shade of green as mine.

"What seems to be the problem, sir?" the lady asked. She wasn't just a lady, though—she was my mother, and the man was my father!

"Maria, Ben, meet your daughter, Emma," Colonel James declared.

They looked stunned and stood there. All of a sudden, they walked toward me and embraced me in a hug.

"I can't believe it's really you!" my dad said. I was thinking the same thing. It was all coming so quickly—I realized that if my parents were alive, then what Colonel James had been saying about magic was true. I was a rune caster. My parents. It was too much to handle – I had so many unanswered questions.

"Oh, honey, you don't know how happy we are to see you! You're so beautiful and grown up!" My mom smiled.

"Can I ask you guys a question?" I asked.

"Anything," my dad replied.

"Where were you? Didn't you want me?" I asked.

"Of course we wanted you!" my mom said. "We loved you with all our hearts."

"Then why did you leave me?" I asked.

"Twila took you out for ice cream. We got a call from the hospital saying you had been hurt. We rushed there, but it was too late, the doctors said you were already dead. We now know that wasn't true and Twila had used a powerful rune to make it appear you were dead. It must've been a powerful rune for we even held a funeral for you with an open casket," my mom told me.

"But Aunt Twila told me that you had died in a car crash. She's been taking care of me for the last eight years!" I said.

"Since Twila is an evil rune caster, I doubt that she's been taking very good care of you, Ms. Emma," Colonel James blurted.

"What is it with all this rune casting and Deliverer stuff?" I asked.

"You've read *Harry Potter*, right?" he asked. I nodded. "Rune casters are like wizards. We cast spells using rocks with runes carved in it, to summon magic, like the one you were holding when we found you. If a rune caster puts his or her hands on a rune and rubs the rune, it activates a spell. You can then throw it or hold it in your hand, facing the rune away from you. This is the light rune casting compound, or as we like to call it, Ebonhaunt. There are five sectors: the training sector, the medical sector, the government sector, the living sector, and the community sector," Colonel James explained. "Anyway, your training will start tomorrow at 9:00 sharp, so be up and ready. You will be placed with kids your age who have been training since they were eight, but you're the Deliverer, so it shouldn't be hard for you to catch up."

"So I'm the most powerful rune caster in the world, or as you guys call it, the Deliverer?"

"Yes, but there's more to it," the Colonel said. "You are only the fourth Deliverer. A Deliverer comes around every two hundred years. There are good and bad Deliverers. You being good or bad, or as we say light or dark, is up to you. Deliverers are born when there is strong light and strong dark in the family. All the Deliverers have left huge marks on history."

"But how can Aunt Twila have done this to me?" I exclaimed. "She seemed so nice!"

"Oh, honey." My mom sat down next to me and rubbed my back. "She was just trying to influence you so that you would choose to be a dark rune caster when you found out about your powers—if you ever did find out," she explained in a soothing voice. The news was just another brick crushing me. It was all too much. Why couldn't I just be a normal person in a nice house with normal friends?

"I think I'm going to go to my room, wherever that is. This is a lot to take in." I rose from my mom's arms.

"I can show her to a room," My mom said to Colonel James. He nodded. "I can't believe you're actually here, my sweet baby girl," my mom said tearing up. I couldn't believe I was here either.

"Well, we can let you take a bed in our room. There's a door separating it from ours. We usually use it as a guest room, but we can re-create it into the perfect room for you!" My dad said excitedly.

"There's so much to learn about you; what you like, what you've been doing all these years!" My mom said as we walked down the halls. The halls were not so welcoming. There were cement walls and floors. The only decoration was the blue rugs that stretched through every hall.

"Yeah, w-we have quite a bit of catching up to do," I stuttered. I couldn't believe I was talking to my mom—I mean, my actual *mother*.

"So what's your life like? What are your hobbies?" my mom asked.

"Well, I work at a restaurant. I'm just a waitress, but I love to cook. I was hoping to work my way up to head chef. I also do track and field and volleyball," I told her.

"You got the cooking from me. I love to cook, too. Two days before Christmas, my mother—your grandma—would bake gingerbread. When I smelled the smell of ginger, I would run to the kitchen to help." She giggled at the memory.

We stopped in front of a door. "This is it," she said. "Of course, it will only be your room for tonight. Then you'll start sleeping in the trainee room."

I walked in and plopped onto the bed. "The schedule and the map are on the wall." My mom pointed. Then, more gently, she asked, "Do you want me to stay here?"

"No, it's okay," I replied. She walked out of the room. The last thing I remember is setting my phone alarm for 7:30 and then drifting off to sleep.

Chapter 4 - Training

Beep-beep. I moved my hand over to the side table to turn off my alarm and got out of bed. I realized that I didn't have any clothes to wear. Heck, I didn't even change into pajamas last night. Did they even get any of my stuff? There was a closet in here—hopefully, it had something. If not, I would have to wear my mom's clothes, and based on her outfit yesterday, I had a feeling I would be wearing leather. I opened the closet, and it was filled with clothes—*my* clothes! It also had boxes. I opened one, and it was filled with my stuff. I grabbed some shorts and a lace white tank top with a loose cardigan and put them on. I looked at the clock. It was 7:35. According to the schedule, I had ten minutes until breakfast.

I stopped for a second. It was weird—I was doing a whole different morning routine, but somehow, it felt normal, as if I had done it a million times. Why was I not freaking out? I mean, I had just found out that I was a powerful rune caster, my parents were alive, and the very person who had raised me was evil. This felt like a dream. Was it? I pinched myself. No, not a dream.

I had to find my way to the dining hall. After five minutes, I just gave up and asked. I opened the door to the dining hall and everybody stared at me. They all wore black leather. Hopefully, I wouldn't have to be wearing that anytime soon. I probably stood out with my different clothes. The dining hall was huge—it had about forty long metal tables, complete with benches and a big line where people got their food like at a school cafeteria. The ceiling and walls were painted blue with white clouds. I wondered why.

"Hello, Emma," Colonel James said.

I jumped. "Um, hi! Colonel James, you scared me!" I exclaimed.

"Follow me." He guided me toward the line. "This is where you will pick up your food for breakfast, lunch, and dinner. You will be escorted every morning from breakfast to the training session," he explained. "So eat quickly." He then turned and left. I stood in line waiting for my food. I felt awkward. It seemed like every pair of eyes in this room was staring at me. When my eyes scanned past my mom and dad, they smiled and waved. I forced a smile. After all, I didn't want to get too excited. This could likely only be a dream.

After I had finished eating, I sat and waited until Colonel James got up onto the stage and started talking. "May I have your attention, please?" he asked. Everybody kept on talking. "I said, may I have your attention, please!" he yelled. Everyone went silent. "Thank you. As you all know, yesterday was finally the day we found the Deliverer. I assure you—you will not be disappointed. I would like to introduce you to the Deliverer: Emma Westley!" Everyone clapped. "Emma, will you please come up to the stage?" he asked. I stood and walked to the stage. It seemed as if a million eyes followed me and every footstep of mine was being judged.

"Meet the Deliverer!" the Colonel exclaimed. Everybody clapped and whooped. I blushed and gazed out into the crowd, looking for my mom and dad. I found them and waved. They waved back.

Everyone was still clapping for me. I had never had this many people clap for me before. It was amazing! "Settle down, settle down!" James called. "You are dismissed." I walked back to my seat.

A girl about my age with long black hair and deep blue eyes was sitting next to me. "So *you're* the Deliverer," she greeted. "Well, that explains your outift." I giggled. "I'm Kiara," she went on. "Nice to meet you."

"I'm Emma," I replied.

"We'll be in the same training group, because I'm sixteen, too," she told me.

"Cool," I commented.

The boy sitting next to me now beamed. "Wow, you're the Deliverer! Nice to meet you, it's an honor!" The boy had brown hair, brown eyes, and freckles on his nose.

"Oh, come on, Luke, she's not the queen!" Kiara teased the boy.

"Luke? I've never heard that name before," I remarked.

"You haven't?" Kiara exclaimed. "I know like ten people with that name! Of course, it's one of the most common rune caster names."

A man with sleek black hair and a tattoo of a dragon on his arm came through the dining hall door. "All sixteen-year-old trainees, please follow me to the trainee room," he stated.

"Let's go," Kiara said to Luke and me.

As we walked into the trainee room, my eyes popped. The floor was covered in gymnastics mats, and one wall was covered in weapons all the way from knives to bows and arrows. On the wall across from the weapons, the only things I could see were buckets and buckets of runes. All the runes were like the one I saw in the parking lot with the glowing symbol in a rock.

"Where do they get all these runes?" I whispered to Kiara.

"The rune yard, of course," she replied. I had no idea what that was, but I just went along with it. A woman walked into the room. She looked about 22. She wore black leather like everyone else, and she had blonde hair and blue eyes.

"Welcome," she said. "I am Marissa. I will be your new trainer. Now, everybody line up according to height." We all scrambled. "Any questions?" she asked. I was still standing next to Kiara since we had similar heights, and now a little boy with wide blue eyes was standing to the right of me.

A girl with curly red hair raised her hand. Every person in the room stared at her. You could tell she was trying not to make eye contact for her brown eyes were scanning the floor.

"What happened to our old trainer?" She asked in a gentle quivering voice. I wondered why she seemed so uneasy.

"There have been some new students added to the class. Your previous trainer did not feel comfortable with some of these new students," Marissa explained. *Wait the old trainer didn't want me to be in his class; after all I was the only new student? Who was the old trainer?*

"That's because our old trainer was the Deliverer's father. He didn't feel uncomfortable; it's against the rules!" I heard a boy mutter.

"What rule?" I whispered to Kiara.

"You can't be trained or schooled by anyone related to you," Kiara whispered back.

"But, what about homeschooling?" I asked her.

"Homeschooling?" Kiara answered sounding very confused. I had forgotten she hadn't grown up in the human world and didn't know these terms. The people here probably had a different name for it.

"You know, when you stay at your home and your parents or a private teacher teach you what you would learn in school," I explained. Kiara's eyes bulged like I was telling her about aliens.

"You mean in the human world you can learn at home! I wish they had that here, but here you're required to start schooling when you're eight in casting classes. Then you have to start physical training at eleven. Finally, we start human studies when we're fifteen. The training and schooling doesn't stop until we turn twenty-four," Kiara explained.

"Girls, quiet down. Save your conversation for lunch," Marissa snapped at Kiara and me. I gave Kiara an apologetic look and she smiled.

A boy with shaggy brown hair and evil green eyes raised his hand. Marissa looked at him and he started talking.

"Um, I'm not going to be taught by a girl. What are you going to teach us, how to put on battle makeup?" He snickered with his friends.

"That's Jeremy." Kiara whispered to me leaning across the two people next to me.

"You think that you can teach this class better than me?" Marissa demanded. "I'll make you a deal. I'll fight you, and if you beat me, you can teach this class."

"Deal," Jeremy said.

"But if I win, you will be in charge of lunch cleanup for a week," Marissa finished.

"But that's like 1,000 people!" he whined.

"Well then, you better hope you win."

"No problem," he bragged, "you're just a weak little girl. I could beat you with my eyes closed."

They headed to the mats in the middle of the room. Once they were there. Jeremy through a punch at Marissa but she dodged it and grabbed his arm. Marissa rammed her knee forward and Jeremy flipped. His back smacked the mat and it made a large clapping noise that made everyone wince. He groaned and rolled over. He tried to stand up but fell back down. Marissa towered over him and snickered, "See you at lunch."

She turned to the rest of the class. "Okay, back to training— unless anyone else would like to be stupid and cocky." She started to put us into pairs. I was put with the boy who was standing to the right of me. "The person next to you is who you will be fighting today," Marissa informed us. "The goal is to knock the other person down. Once they are knocked down, you cannot touch them anymore. Got it?" Everybody nodded. "Good," she said.

"Wait, we're not using pads!" I exclaimed shocked to Kiara.

"Nope, I had Marissa a couple years back. She says it's good to get used to the pain. She sees us as adults once we are in training." Kiara explained. I had a feeling this might be a tough trainer to be with.

"Now, who's going first? Hmm, how about you two?" She pointed to Kiara and her partner. "How about Kiara and Margaret?"

Kiara's partner was equal in height but probably weighed about twice as much as her and had bulging muscles. I gulped. There was no way Kiara could beat her! I hoped the girl just pinned her down so Kiara didn't get hurt, but Kiara did not seem like the type of person who would go down without a fight.

The two girls made their way to the mat, and I crossed my fingers. "Ready…go!" Marissa yelled. Margaret threw a punch but Kiara ducked and kicked Margaret's legs. Margaret punched Kiara in the chin, but then Kiara punched Margaret in the face. Margaret fell and rolled over.

"Kiara is the winner!" Marissa exclaimed, holding Kiara's hand up. Everybody clapped. Kiara walked back to where we were waiting and wiped some of the blood off her chin. "I hate going against Margaret. Everyone knows she's the easiest person to fight,"

Kiara muttered to me. I gulped. *The easiest person?* She seemed pretty vicious to me.

Suddenly, the intercom blared. It was Colonel James's voice.

"Everyone please report to the cafeteria immediately! This is an emergency!"

Emergency! For rune casters that didn't sound good.

An alarm started going off, and Marissa got this panicky look on her face. The boy who I was supposed to fight looked like he might throw up. Marissa opened the door and said, "You heard him. Immediately! Come on, let's go!" Everybody started to walk quickly out the door. What was happening?

Chapter 5 - Darkness Arrives

My mind tried to process a blur of questions. All of the people in the rune-casting compound were now crowded into the cafeteria. The room came to a hush as Colonel James walked onto the stage. "We are not sure what is going on, but dark magic was sensed inside the compound," he announced. "To ensure everyone's safety, a spell covering the cafeteria is scanning everyone here. If dark magic is sensed on you, the color of your skin will temporarily change to red. Please stay calm while the spell checks over you."

A woman wearing all black stood up, and I realized that she was my aunt. Before I could think, she whipped off her hoodie to reveal the tattoos that the people at the restaurant had. I ducked right when she cast a spell. A blue rope floated quickly toward me. I ran, but it was too fast. The rope wrapped around me and pulled me to my aunt. Before I knew it, we were bursting through the roof of the compound into the sky. I looked at Twila and she waved her hand. Slowly everything went black, and the last thing I remember is staring into her eyes as we stood on the roof together.

I woke up on a pile of blankets in a concrete room. Across from me was a glowing red door. Then all of the memories of what had happened came rushing through my head. *Where was I? How could I escape?* I wondered. My aunt—the women who had cared for me for half of my life—had captured me. I knew she was a dark rune caster, and the thought of her harming me sent chills through my body. Everything had happened so quickly these past few days that I hadn't had time to process it. But now that I could think about it, the events weighed down on me like a ton of bricks. My aunt finally walked in. I couldn't help but feel scared.

"Hello, Emma, you have no idea how pleased I am to see you again. I am not going to hurt you, because I want you to take in what I am about to say to you. But I do want you to know that I can kill you at any time I want or need to. Your choice to harm the dark rune casters one day will affect whether you or your loved ones are alive the next day. Since the first spark of magic, light rune casters have done nothing but harm innocent rune casters. They label us as dark, when they are the ones hurting people!" She was still treating me like a child, after everything I had been through!

I started to yell, "Innocent? How can you claim to be innocent! You told me my parents were dead! You are horrid!" I lunged at her and tried to hit her with everything I had.

My aunt waved her arm, making me fly across the room and crash into the wall. A pain jolted through my left arm.

I began to stutter, "H-how did you d-do that? Don't you need runes to cast?"

"You can harness this power, too, Emma, if you let me teach you," Aunt Twila explained. "You can have so much power!"

"Never!" I replied.

"Make sure you know just how light those close to you are," my aunt said. She waved her hand like she had before. Once again everything went black.

Chapter 6 - Stay Hidden

When I woke up, I was lying in my bed in the compound. My parents told me that I was there at night when they got back from work. They said that the search party sent out for me hadn't returned yet, and I wondered how I had come back myself. When they asked what had happened to me, I didn't want them to know I was scared of my loved ones being hurt if I harmed the dark Runecasters, so I left parts out. If my parents knew about that, they would go after Aunt Twila, and most likely not return like the search party.

So I told them, "Aunt Twila captured me. She explained that her powers could hurt me—probably to scare me."

"Well, we're just glad that you're safe," my father replied.

"How did this happen?" my mother said, indicating my left arm. I looked and saw a bandage wrapped around it. I remembered Aunt Twila throwing me against the wall with her spell.

"Oh…I slipped and fell on my arm," I lied. I couldn't believe that Twila had hurt me, and I didn't want to share the fact that she did!

Suddenly, there was a knock on the door. "Come in," my mom said. "We have to get going," she commented to me. "We have a mission to work on. Usually, we would not let you go, because it's dangerous. But, we actually need you to do this."

"What mission?" I asked.

"You'll know soon enough," my dad replied as Kiara and Luke entered.

"We have to go sweetie. Kiara and Luke can show you around while your father and I are at the council meeting," my mom said, as my parents exited the room.

"I heard what happened. Was it scary? What were the aliens like?" Luke asked.

"Wait—aliens?" I wondered.

"Yah, we heard you were abducted by aliens," he answered.

"What? Aliens didn't abduct me! Whoever you heard that from was very wrong," I said.

Kiara and Luke broke out laughing. "We were joking, but we are sorry about what happened," Luke laughed.

"The council was in a meeting until you came back. They just started another one," Kiara said.

"The council?" I wondered.

"I can't believe you don't know!' Luke exclaimed. "Your and Kiara's parents are on it. It's like the Ebonhaunt government."

"Oh. Why have they been meeting for so long?" I asked.

"I don't know," Luke said. "My mom said they haven't had a meeting this long since she was a young girl, and those were very bad times."

"I think I know a way to figure out why they're meeting," Kiara said.

I got a little worried. I had only known Kiara for a short period of time, and she seemed a little daring.

She continued, "If we go to the work sector where the council meets, there's a window where you can hear what they're saying and see the council members. I've been doing it since I was little when I was bored."

"I don't know about this," I said nervously. "We could get in trouble."

"Trust me," Kiara answered. Since she was one of my only two friends, I went with her, even though I knew I would most likely regret it later.

Chapter 7 - We Can't Know

When we got to the work sector, Kiara instructed us to tell anyone who asked that Luke and she were giving me a tour of the compound. Surprisingly, our walking confidently through the sector where children weren't supposed to go actually worked. When we got to the room, we crowded our heads along the window to get a good view of the council. My dad was standing up, saying, "But Twila's necklace could be too powerful if it fell into the wrong hands, and as long as she's alive, the necklace will have its power. There's no way to do this without Plan Fern."

"What's that?" I whispered.

"They have code names for all their plans," Kiara answered. I wondered what Plan Fern was but guessed that Kiara and Luke wouldn't know.

A lady in a business suit stood up and said, "So it's set. We have to have Emma kill Twila."

I gulped and started to breathe heavily. Before I knew it, I was crying. I felt like I had swallowed a brick. A fat man wandered over near the window with his back turned to us—I immediately didn't like him. Everybody was leaving, so I figured we should head back to our rooms. But at that moment, the man turned around, saw us, and yelled, "Aah! Children!"

We jumped back and ran to the doorway, but my parents and Kiara's mom got there first.

"You kids are in big trouble" Kiara's mom said to us. We stepped out into the hall to face our parents.

"Why on earth would you spy on the council?" my dad snapped. "Some of what we were talking about is top secret. How much did you hear?"

The man who spotted us was walking down the hallway muttering, "Filthy, wretched little children."

"Why is *he* allowed on the council to know this top secret information?" Luke criticized.

"That's not the point. How much did you hear?" My dad directed this toward me.

"I won't kill her. She raised me. She wiped my tears when I fell down. She tucked me into bed," I said.

"She killed hundreds of people! She killed members of our family!" my dad yelled.

"Honey, settle down," my mom quieted him.

"Who?" I gasped.

"What?" my mom asked.

"Who did she kill?" I answered.

"It doesn't matter," my mom replied.

"Who?"

Kiara and Luke looked worried that I was screaming.

"She killed—she killed her own mother. She killed my mother—your grandmother," my mom whispered.

"But why?" I wondered.

31

"To become a dark rune caster and prove you are really evil, you have to kill a member of your family," my mom said quietly. "Our whole family had all been members of the light rune casters' council. But there was always something different about Twila—she would skip classes and steal my toys when I was little. When she was sixteen, Twila decided to become dark and knew our mother wouldn't approve. So rather than cause our mother the grief of raising a dark rune caster, Twila killed her. Her committing this action was what truly darkened her soul."

"Wouldn't your mother have rather lived with that grief than die?" I asked.

"Sometimes, pain is worse than death," my mother answered.

"It's just too hard. I'll do what is best for the Ebonhaunt community," I said.

"That's killing Twila," my mom told me. "That's your mission, Emma, and you must succeed in order to protect Ebonhaunt."

Chapter 8 - New Adventure

Once my mom, dad, and I got back to their room, they started explaining the mission. But I couldn't avoid the disappointed stares they gave me for spying on them. I had just come to know my parents and I had already disappointed them.

"This mission will be dangerous. The dark rune casters' lair has systems to spot planes, and a car would need a lot of gas to function, so we will be walking. This is the only time it comes in handy that the dark rune casters put their lair near ours to attack us. Another challenge is that once we leave the compound, we are no longer under a protection spell. The dark rune casting lair is also heavily guarded, but luckily, they do not have a protection spell. Only light runecasters can cast protection spells."

"Wait, what's so important about Twila's necklace?" I asked.

"It belongs to the leader of the dark rune casters and allows them to cast powerful dark spells. It also allows them to cast without any runes," my dad said.

"Why do *I* have to kill Twila? Why can't someone else kill her?" I wondered.

"Only the Deliverer can kill a dark leader," my mom said. I understood now that there was no getting out of it. But would this be considered an act of defying dark rune casters like what Twila was talking about? "You will also get to select two strong trainees your age to join the mission group. In two days, there will be a ceremony at which the compound will learn about your mission and you will announce the mission members. We will give you a list of the five already selected members plus you and your two trainees."

I already knew whom I was going to choose. Really, my only two options were Luke and Kiara. I knew they could do it. Luke was smart, and Kiara was clever.

"I've decided on my two trainees," I said.

"Oh, it's not like that," my mom said. "There are auditions for your trainees tomorrow."

"Um…Luke is in room 213 and Kiara is in 327, right?" I asked.

"We alerted Luke's parents about what happened tonight and Kiara's mom was there, so they're probably in trouble, but you can check," my dad said.

"Yes! Thank you," I replied.

Once I got to Kiara's room, I knocked on the door.

"Hello." Kiara's mom answered the door. She opened it enough for me to see Kiara sitting angrily on her bed.

"Hi, could I speak to Kiara?" I asked.

"Sorry, but Kiara is not allowed visitors right now," her mom replied.

"Please, it's important, and it can't wait," I pleaded.

"Fine, you have ten minutes," her mom announced.

"Tomorrow, I have auditions for two trainees to join me on a mission to kill Twila," I told Kiara.

"Oh…" she said, seeming concerned. "I wouldn't be good enough," she spat out.

"Yes, you would, and you're one of the only two people I would trust with this mission. Please audition," I begged.

"Okay, fine. But you'll see what I mean when I don't make it," she said.

"And you'll see what I mean when you do make it," I asserted.

Next was Luke, and he had already made plans to audition. Now all I needed was for them to do great in the auditions, but I had never seen them rune cast before. What if the other judges decided they weren't good enough? I would just have to wait until tomorrow.

When I got to auditions the next day, the setup was explained to me. Two other judges—Colonel James and Marissa—and I would judge the one hundred contestants on two different tasks: casting and knowledge. In the casting challenge, each contestant would use one rune he or she picked out to destroy a dummy. In the knowledge challenge, contestants would be given a test regarding what to do in certain situations. At the end, the judges would review their notes to decide who would join me on the mission.

After about forty contestants, it was Kiara's turn. I was so nervous for her that I was shaking.

"What rune did you choose, Ms. Kiara?" Colonel James asked.

"I chose the rune of movement," Kiara answered. I got worried. Nobody who had succeeded so far had chosen that rune. I watched as Kiara began to cast. She lifted up the two tables on opposite sides of the room so they were vertical and began to close

35

them in on the dummy. All of a sudden she slammed the two tables together with the dummy in the middle. The dummy fell down as flat as a piece of paper. I was excited. Kiara was actually doing really well. We excused her and wrote down some notes about her.

When Luke came up, I wasn't so worried for him after Kiara's great performance. I knew he would do great.

"I have chosen the boulder rune," Luke stated. He cast a boulder and threw it at the metal dummy, denting it. Marissa shook her head and excused him.

I watched through a glass window as many kids sat in rows scribbling on their papers. It was the knowledge test.

After the knowledge test results came in, Colonel James, Marissa, and I sat down to discuss the contestants.

"I really liked Luke and Kiara," I said, trying to sound casual.

"Kiara was very good, but Luke isn't quite ready. We want the people on the mission to be well trained and prepared," Marissa commented.

"I agree with Marissa. Luke isn't ready," Colonel James said. I began to get butterflies in my stomach. Luke had to make it. He had to.

"We have other well-trained team members. Won't it be okay if one member just needs a little more training?" I argued.

"One weed can kill a beautiful garden," Marissa stated.

"Luke isn't a weed!" I exclaimed.

"This group needs to be perfect," Marissa explained, trying to settle me down. "As much as I hate to say this," she went on, "we have a great contestant in Jeremy." I was surprised. Jeremy had totally sassed her the other day in class. "I think Kiara and Jeremy would be wise choices for the two trainees," Marissa concluded. "All in favor of these two trainees raise their hands."

Colonel James and Marissa raised their hands. After a few moments, I decided to raise my hand, too. I was assigned to post the results. On the walk down the hallway, which was crowded with contestants, I tried to avoid eye contact with Luke. When he gave me a hopeful glance, I felt like I had been shrunk down to the size of an ant. When I hung the results, I waited 'til Luke saw the paper. When he came up, I got a sick feeling in my stomach and felt like I was going to cry. I knew how much he wanted this.

Once he read the paper, he looked at me and smiled. "It's okay, maybe next time." He shrugged.

"I'm sorry," I apologized. "I tried to get you a spot. I couldn't. I'm sorry. I get my first two rune caster friends, and I betray one."

"You didn't betray me," Luke assured me. "I'm glad to have a friend like you who sticks up for other people. You tried as hard as you could, and that's all that matters."

Chapter 9 - The Departure

My parents had picked out an outfit to wear for the ceremony and my departure. I was wearing a baby blue dress for the ceremony. For the departure, I would wear a lightweight jacket over a short-sleeved shirt and parachute pants. The compound hairstylist had done my hair into a bun with a curly hairpiece on top. I was as ready as I'd ever be.

I walked up the steps to the stage of the compound. I was nervous and tried to hide that I was shaking. It was finally my turn to speak. I began to say what I had rehearsed, "On this mission to benefit the lives of the light rune casters, I set out to kill the dark leader. Wise, strong, and brave people join me on this mission. Colonel James, Marissa Tittens, Ben Westley, Maria Westley, Kiara Findows, and Jeremy Finner, please come to the stage."

I stepped back with the line of my team members and put my head down like them. The compound began to speak in unison, "We, the light rune casters of Ebonhaunt, wish you the wisdom of the great owl, the stealth of the monkey, the strength of this whole compound, and the bravery you will need. We wish you luck."

I felt like my stomach was doing flips. The chant had made the journey seem a lot more dangerous than I already thought it was. I was now more worried for my friends and myself. After the chant, I could see Kiara shaking and Jeremy gulping.

I tried to fight a smile when I saw my parents holding each other's hands. It reminded me of the picture at my house of them holding each other's hands walking in a field. I never thought I would get to see it in real life. I also never thought that I would believe in magic.

My team members and I lifted our heads. I looked out at the compound audience. They were all staring at us. Usually, I would get stage fright, but I felt too connected to these people, so I stared right back and smiled. When I got off the stage, my parents took my hand.

"Good job, honey," my dad congratulated.

"We got you a gift," my mom said, "to not only congratulate you on this but also on the beautiful girl you have become. We are so proud of you." She handed me a wrapped gift. I ripped open the paper to find a picture frame. I flipped it over and saw a picture of my parents holding me as a baby. I reached over and hugged my parents.

"Thank you," I said. My eyes started to tear up. I only wished that I had more pictures like this.

"Come on, let's go back to the room," my mom said.

Once we got back to the room, I changed into my clothes for the departure. I grabbed my backpack for the mission and started to put my things into it. I wrapped the picture my parents had given me in my clothes and put it in my backpack. My mom and dad came into the room.

"Are you ready?" my mom asked.

I swung my backpack on my shoulders and said, "I'm ready."

At the doors to the compound, Colonel James gave us instructions. "Once we get past the protection spell barriers, it will be dangerous. We will be possible victims of dark rune casters. But the people on this mission have been carefully selected, so I trust that we will be prepared if anything happens."

"We have also secured transporters inside your bag on the bottom," Marissa told me.

"What are transporters?" I asked.

"They let you transport one thing to a different place without even touching it. For instance, I put rune bracelets on my transporter, so they appeared on your transporters in your bags." Marissa explained. At the bottom of my bag, I found a metal disk with a glowing blue circle in the middle. On top of it was a bracelet. I pulled out the bracelet, and along with everyone else, put mine on.

"I've heard of these but never really knew what they were. How does this work?" Kiara asked.

"Our compound scientists made them," Marissa said. "We shrunk down runes and laced them onto strong fabric. Now you can cast without even picking up a rune. The bracelet has almost all the runes on it—they're just microscopic. Think of what you want to cast, and then cast it."

"Wow, this is so cool. I've got to try this out!" Jeremy exclaimed and then formed a water droplet in his hand.

"Well, we do have a schedule, so we better stick to it," Colonel James said hurriedly. The doors opened, and we walked out. This was the first time I had been outside in days. The compound safety barriers were two statues about fifty feet away. Outside the compound, there was a beautiful garden full of flowers and trees.

"Are these flowers real?" I asked, pointing to a flower that was swaying and changing colors.

"They're as real as magic," Jeremy said. "I can't believe you haven't seen a *coloria* flower before! They're what we use to make a lot of the compound sauces." As everyone resumed walking toward the barrier, I marveled at the amazing garden around me. Somehow, these plants seemed just as alive as animals.

"Here we are," Colonel James said as we reached the barrier. I watched as my team members began to move forward. Then I looked back at the compound and took a step, crossing the barrier myself.

Chapter 10 - It Begins

"If you look back, the compound will appear to be gone," Colonel James said. "This is because of the protection spell. Now if we meet anyone along the way, we are just people exploring the great outdoors."

"Now, let's move!" Marissa commanded. "This is a long journey, and we don't have a lot of time before the dark rune casters figure out where we are and what we are doing."

We began to jog in a group, Marissa leading us. We entered a meadow filled with dark purple flowers.

"You're killing the woman who raised you," someone mysteriously whispered.

"Who said that?" I asked nervously. Everyone looked at each other, trying to see who had spoken.

"Jeremy and his dad—or no dad?" another whisper came. I saw Jeremy's face go blank.

"You left behind your only daughter with the most evil rune caster," something else whispered.

"Welcome to the whispering meadows," Colonel James said. "Cover your ears, everyone! The plants will whisper your worst nightmares. In this case, words really can kill!"

"It's not working, I can still hear them!" Jeremy yelled, crying.

"Everyone huddle in," Marissa said. "I'm going to cast a protection spell."

We huddled in, and a bubble formed around us. The sound waves began to bounce off the bubble, and everything went silent. But in a minute, the sound waves began to push against the bubble until it popped. It seemed like the plants were screaming all my worries, fears, and anxieties at me. I knelt down and held my hands to my ears, but the plants just got louder and louder.

"We have to get out of here!" I heard my dad yell.

Kiara and Jeremy were in the same position as I was. Jeremy slowly stood up, along with Kiara, but I couldn't—it was too loud. It was really scary to hear everything bad about my life at once. I could see everyone covering their ears, running toward the exit of the meadows.

"Just lie down and close your eyes, and it will all be over," I heard one of the plants whisper.

Jeremy turned around and saw me. He put his arms through my elbows and carried me with him.

"I can still hear them! Put me down! Put me down, so it can be over!" I was screaming at Jeremy. He kept on running. The group was staggering in different directions.

"It will be over in just a few more feet," Jeremy tried to reassure me.

"I want it to be over now!" I cried. Then Jeremy jumped, diving out of the meadow, and everything went quiet.

The other members of our group were not there. I was breathing hard and trying to stop crying. I could still hear the whispers echoing through my mind. I curled up, crying, on the ground.

"Everyone else went out different ways. We should try to find them," Jeremy suggested.

"Why didn't you put me down? I wanted it to be over. Why couldn't you have put me down?" I sobbed.

"Because you would've died, Emma. The plants would've killed you. Just be thankful you're still alive. I could've left you there!" Jeremy shot back.

"Thank you," I said.

"I only did it because the mission would be over if you died," Jeremy said quickly. I stood up and brushed dirt off my pants.

"Why do you ask for affection and admiration and then just push it all away when you get it?" I blurted.

"I'd rather not talk about it," Jeremy said.

"Fine," I said. "We better start looking for the other team members. I'd prefer to spend as little time as possible alone with you."

"Okay, let's go," Jeremy replied.

We began to walk along the border of the top of the meadow.

"We're never going to find them—this meadow is super long!" Jeremy complained.

"They have to be here somewhere. They couldn't have staggered off too far," I asserted.

"Emma, Jeremy!" someone shouted. We looked diagonally right and saw Kiara and Marissa in the distance. They ran to us and stopped.

"We've been looking all over for you! Where have you been?" Marissa exclaimed.

"Looking for you," I answered. "How did you get out of the meadow?"

Kiara began to answer but then Jeremy interrupted, "It's not a high school reunion. Come on, let's get moving, we still have four people to find."

"Well, someone's not having a good day," Kiara muttered.

"And you are?" Jeremy yelled at Kiara. "Tiny little weak flowers just shouted out all your fears, worries, and regrets to you. And you couldn't stop it! It seems like I was the only person who did anything useful in the meadows. I got Emma out for this mission, for the light rune casters. I could've died today and might tomorrow!"

Kiara gave me a worried glance. "We came out with everyone else. We were about to start looking for you two, so Marissa and I climbed to the top of a tree to see if we saw you. That was when dark rune casters attacked. They came from all directions on the ground. I tried to help, but Marissa and I realized we weren't strong enough. There were too many of them. So Marissa cast a temporary protection spell around us so we couldn't be seen by the dark rune casters."

"We have to help!" I exclaimed. "I mean, it's my parents and Colonel James!"

"They have been captured," Marissa said. "We will find them at the dark rune casters' lair. We will split up. Emma will go after Twila, and I will find our friends. I know where to go, but sadly, since the dark rune casters know where we are, we will have to take the longer route in the human world. I have had human clothes from the compound sent through our transmitters, so I suggest we change now."

I opened my backpack and pulled out jeans and a Rolling Stones T-shirt. I walked behind a bush and changed into the new clothes. I took my hairpiece out and brushed my hair into a ponytail. I came out to see that everyone else was changed and looked like people from my old school.

"Okay, everyone strap your backpacks on tight. I'm going to cast a portal to the human world," Marissa ordered. She waved her hand, and a portal appeared. It was an oval with a clear view of a city. Floating on top of the portal were the words *New York City*. Marissa jumped in.

"Going to die one day anyway," Kiara said and then jumped in. Jeremy jumped in next, and it was my turn. I jumped, ready for a hard fall, but I ended up only dropping about a foot.

We were now all standing in a deserted alleyway. Straight ahead, there were tall buildings and lots of lights. I was surprisingly happy to be back in the human world. I had thought that Ebonhaunt was a place that I'd never want to leave.

"The compound messaged me, telling me to use a bus, and gave me a bus schedule," Marissa declared. "Emma, where's this bus they speak of, and what will it do?"

"You don't know what a bus is? It takes you places around the city," I told her.

"So humans have portals around the city?" Kiara wondered.

"No, buses are vehicles. You check the bus schedule, and it tells you what bus to take to get where you want to go. You wait for the bus to come and then pay to get on. Here, let me see the schedule. Where do we have to go?" I asked.

Marissa handed me the schedule and then said, "We have to go to someplace called Vermont and then New Hampshire."

I opened the bus schedule. "In twenty minutes, about one block away, there's a bus that goes to Vermont. It's about a three-hour ride. Marissa, did you get any money?" I asked.

"Yah, we should all have some in our packs," Marissa replied.

"Well, we better hurry if we're going to make the bus," Jeremy said.

We started to walk, Kiara, Jeremy, and Marissa following my lead. "So remember, guys, no magic!" I reminded them. "Humans will call the police if you use it. The police are people who imprison you if you do something bad." I said to Kiara, "We'll tell people that we're best friends, and Marissa is our older sister. On the bus, talk about music groups."

"Oh, like Fifth Rune! I love that band!" Kiara squealed.

"No, I mean talk about human world music groups, like The Beatles," I suggested.

"I almost forgot. Remember when you studied phones in class, Jeremy and Kiara?" Marissa said. Jeremy and Kiara nodded their heads. "Well, the compound sent smart phones to your transmitters. They already have each of our numbers built in. Now if anyone has any questions on the bus, just text one another." We all pulled out our new phones.

"Here we are," I said as we arrived at the bus stop. "We have about ten minutes until the bus arrives." The bus stop was on an almost empty street, which was saying something for New York. There was a lady sitting on a blue bench waiting for the bus. When it arrived, we filed on to the bus and gave the driver money. We sat down in the back row, as far away as possible from the other four passengers on the bus.

The older lady at the bus stop, who was sitting a row in front of us, turned around and said, "What lovely bracelets you have. What are those rocks on them?"

"Thank you. They're friendship charms," I answered.

"That's wonderful," the lady commented.

"Well, it's nice to meet you. I'm Emma." I introduced myself.

"Oh, I know who you are," she said. "Twila wanted me to send you a very special message. Stay away from the dark rune casters' lair or else your whole compound will regret ever getting involved with us." The bus doors opened and the lady stood up. "It was nice meeting you, Emma, I hope we don't meet again." She walked off the bus. Marissa, Jeremy, Kiara, and I were all exchanging worried glances, so I opened a group text.

Me: *I thought the dark rune casters couldn't get into or harm the compound.*

Jeremy: *They can't—but they're somehow going to do something that will negatively affect all the people in the compound.*

Kiara: *Like what?*

Marissa: *I think she is going to hurt Colonel James. The light rune casters' government will collapse without a leader.*

Me: *We have to help him!*

Marissa: *We're going as fast as we can!*

Me: *Why didn't Twila just capture us?*

Marissa: *Because she knows you are a danger to her.*

Kiara: *So do we still go?*

Marissa: *They know where we are now, but I'm casting a spell so they can't follow our location. But we'd better hurry. It will only take a week or so before the dark rune casters realize we haven't gone back to the compound.*

Me: *So we're still going.*

Marissa: *Yes, but we'd best be cautious.*

Jeremy: *I don't know about you, but I'm going to get some sleep.*

Me: *I don't know if I'll be able to after the things that have happened today.*

Kiara: *Me, either*

Marissa: *You can go to sleep, Jeremy, but we're going to do some more planning. Kiara, I hear you're pretty tech savvy. Would you be able to find the locations of the captured?*

Kiara: *Working on it right now.*

Marissa: *All right. Kiara and I will go get the captured, and Emma and Jeremy will go after Twila.*

Jeremy: *You're right, I couldn't sleep. I'm good with that plan.*

Marissa: *Then it's final. Kiara, how far are you on those locations?*

Kiara: *I managed to hack into their network. Maria and Ben are on the second floor in room 5349 and Colonel James is in room 5350. I also pulled up a map of the lair and a secret entrance used in the olden days by light rune casters to sneak in.*

Jeremy: *I think we're at the stop.*

Me: *Okay, let's get off now.*

We all stood up and put away our phones. We exited the bus with our backpacks. In front of us was a car rental place.

"So what now?" I asked Marissa.

"We have to rent a car," she answered.

"Well, *that's* convenient," I said motioning to the car rental place.

"I may have made a few alterations in the bus driver's mind to come here next," Marissa admitted.

"How much money did the compound give us? A car rental is expensive." I said.

"As much as we need," Marissa replied. "Don't worry, we know what cars are. We've used them in Ebonhaunt." We started walking toward the car rental place.

"The compound already reserved the car for us," Marissa said. "We just have to give the car dealers this ticket and pay the fee."

We opened the door to the car dealership. There was a beat-up couch and fish tank to our right and to our left was a desk with two men sitting at it. One man had uneven sideburns and a blue jumpsuit. The other man wore a t-shirt and sagging jeans.

"What can I do for you, miss?" the man with the sagging jeans asked.

"We had a car reserved. Is this where we pick it up?" Marissa replied.

The man with the sagging jeans slipped on a tuxedo jacket and said, "Wonderful, this is where you can pick up that car. I'm Jason, and I'll be helping you today."

The other man began to take piles of papers off the desk and put them on the ground to make it look neat. "Look, miss, we have a busy schedule, so this is how it's going to work," he said. "You're going to give us the money, and we're going to give you the keys to that car over there." He pointed to a big black car. He held out the keys and said, "You're renting it for a week, so that's around seven hundred dollars for the week." Marissa handed him a credit card and then he snatched it. If we hadn't needed the car right now I would've told Marissa we should go somewhere else, these guys were totally ripping us off!

"No keys for you today!" Jason said.

Marissa cast and flung them into the wall. She caught the keys and credit card in midair and then said, "Come on let's get out of here!" We opened the car doors. Marissa and Kiara sat in the front, and Jeremy and I sat in the back.

"Why would you do that?" I yelled at Marissa.

"It's not like they'll know I was using magic," Marissa defended herself.

"But other people might! In the human world, we have security cameras!" I fired back.

"Well, the faster we get out of here, the more likely they wont catch us. If you want Colonel James to be alive when we get to the dark rune casters' lair, we'd better hurry," Marissa said. I leaned back into my seat and crossed my arms.

"Marissa, do you know how to drive?" Kiara asked.

"Don't worry, I cast a spell so the car will move to where we need to go," Marissa said smoothly.

"Well, at least put your hands on the steering wheel so the humans don't wonder why a car is moving without anyone driving," Jeremy criticized.

We started driving toward New Hampshire and I began to worry about what was happening to my parents. If Twila was evil enough to kill her own mother, she was evil enough to hurt her sister and brother-in-law. This car couldn't get me there quick enough! I had finally gotten my parents back—I never thought they would go away again. All of my new life was too crazy to be true. I wasn't entirely sure if I liked it or not.

"Emma, are you okay?" Kiara asked. "You look worried."

"Yes, I'm fine," I answered. They would think I was selfish if I told him that I was worried about my parents instead of being worried for Colonel James.

"Emma, it's time I start training you," Marissa suggested. "Twila is no easy match." I began to get excited. I would finally learn how to use the best of my rune casting abilities. "We should make a stop in about twenty minutes. Kiara, why don't you cast everyone some food?"

Kiara cast me a hot dog, Jeremy a sandwich, Marissa a burger, and a pizza for herself.

"Sorry, my food casting skills aren't the best. Everything may be a little undercooked," she apologized.

"The casting is all so amazing," I admitted. "It's so hard to believe. Sometimes, I'm scared that this is all a dream."

"Well, don't be scared it's a dream, because it's my life's reality," Jeremy commented wryly.

I took a bite into the hot dog. It tasted just like one from a stand in Times Square. I opened my backpack and took out a bottle of water.

"Try making the bottle of water cold. Just concentrate with all your might on a cold water bottle," Jeremy explained. I held the water bottle and thought, *A cold water bottle, nice cold water*. I felt coolness and unscrewed the cap. I took a sip of the water, and it was ice cold. Kiara peered at me. I gave her a thumbs up, and she high-fived me.

"Good job, Jeremy!" Marissa congratulated him. "You taught Emma the basics and it worked. And good job, Emma, you learn quickly!" I smiled, proud of myself, and wished my parents could see this.

"Let's stop here," Marissa said and pulled over the car next to a forest. We hopped out of the car, and Marissa locked it. The forest was filled with trees and looked pretty isolated—a good place to practice magic. Marissa led us over to the forest. We traveled until we were deep in the trees.

"Now, you will need to use fighting runes, which require a sharp mind," Marissa said. She began to tell me what to do. "You need to see the person in pain from whatever spell you are casting. Your hand movements have to be fluid and reflect something about the person. To kill someone by rune casting, you must excel at all these things."

"I'm not sure how I feel about killing someone," I worried.

"Twila has already killed so many and will kill many more if you don't kill her and retrieve the necklace," Marissa reasoned. She cast a panther. The panther slowly moved toward me. "Don't worry, it's fake—it won't hurt you, and it won't actually be harmed," Marissa reassured. "The panther is just an image, not a living creature." I moved my hands as though they were the panther's feet slinking across the ground. I thought of the panther lying down and not breathing. The panther rolled over and did as I thought. Then it vanished.

"You did it!" Kiara squealed. I smiled, proud of myself, but I was secretly scared. I couldn't do that to a living person.

Chapter 11 - Evil

We rode in the car again. I was still pondering the thought of killing Twila. Despite everything she had done, she was family. It didn't make it right for me to kill her just because she killed people. But I had to do it, and there would be no changing it. If I didn't kill her, thousands more would die, and I would be responsible for their deaths.

"Shouldn't Emma learn physical combat, too?" Jeremy suggested.

"We will get to that another day. Don't be so eager for Emma to learn how to punch you in the face!" Marissa snickered. Kiara laughed, and so did I. It was the first time I had laughed in a while. It felt like I had just pushed a weight off my shoulders.

"Just want to make sure the special Deliverer doesn't walk in and get her butt kicked," Jeremy sassed.

I glared at him and shot back, "Because you would care."

Jeremy fired back his answer: "Actually, I *would* care, because if you do get your butt kicked, thousands of people's death—including your own and Colonel James's—will be caused by you. So, for once, stop thinking about how it's going to affect you and think of how it will affect everyone else."

I was ticked off now, so I spoke back without thinking. "You think I'm not thinking about other people? How's this for thinking about other people? Thinking day and night about how my casting skills will affect thousands of people's lives in a negative way. Worrying if I will be able to save Colonel James—not for me, but for other people. Only wondering once if Twila would kill my parents or not, which she probably already has!" Kiara and Marissa looked at me with stunned looks.

Jeremy just looked away, refusing to admit he'd lost the fight.

"You know, Emma," he drawled, "sometimes people do something wrong. Sometimes they do something right. Don't use the things that you do right as a defense when someone tells you things that you did wrong." Jeremy said. I turned away and looked out the window.

"Someone's got some warming up to do," Kiara said, directing her message to Jeremy. I wished it was Luke in that seat next to me, not Jeremy. Sometimes, it may not be about having a skilled team but having a cohesive one. I wished the people at the compound had understood that. The people at the compound only wanted team members on the mission who were skilled at certain magical things. They didn't look at other important things like creativity, cooperation, or teamwork.

"Duck!" Marissa yelled. I heard something hit my window but nothing came into the car.

"I have a protection spell on the car, but it wont be there for long!" Marissa said. She took the steering wheel herself and turned off the steering spell. I looked to my right and saw people, but with roots for hair and branches for arms.

"What happened? What's going on?" I yelled nervously at Marissa.

"They're earthkeepers. They have transported us back into the rune casting world, but sadly, they came, too," Marissa replied, jerking the steering wheel to the left and hitting one.

"What are earthkeepers?" I asked.

"I don't really have time to explain!" Marissa shouted back. All I could hear was Marissa yelling and roots cracking.

"Everyone open your windows and start casting!" Marissa ordered. I opened my window and began to cast fire. I missed the first one, but the second time, I was right on target. The earthkeeper burst into flames. I began to try to make their root hair grow into the ground. I imagined their roots growing, planting themselves deep in the earth, and saw that five got stuck. Another one began to run toward me. I tried to cast but couldn't think quickly enough. It was two feet away from me and flashed its pointy teeth. I brought my arms over my head, but then Marissa turned the car, hitting the earthkeeper. Its brown, muddy face was thrown back, and the earthkeeper fell to the ground.

Marissa pulled the car onto a beach, and the earthkeepers seemed to back away, hissing at the edge of the sand. I panted, scared, and said, "What were those things?"

Marissa answered, "A long time ago, human-world trees were planted in a sacred forest by travelers. The light rune casters only wanted magical trees in the sacred forest, because they would pray there. So the light rune casters began to cut down the human-world

58

trees. After hundreds had been chopped down, some light rune casters went to the sacred forest to cut down more. The second that one of the rune casters touched that tree with his ax, a branch grabbed him and pulled him in, suffocating him. The other rune casters tried to help, but it was no use. The tree was too strong. The trees evolved to defend themselves from us. The men returned to Ebonhaunt to tell the then-leader of the compound, Lady Rita, of what had happened. Many other rune casters went and tried again to chop down the trees but none ever returned. So one night Lady Rita went to the circle in the sacred forest to pray with her guards. One guard peered into the forest and saw the first earthkeeper. When the earthkeeper walked, the trees leaned in the opposite direction. The guards hurried Lady Rita to leave, but as they departed, they heard the earthkeeper singing the same song over and over again:

Down with hundreds of our family.

The trees they fell.

Even our own leader was chopped to the ground.

The people who have done this did it mindfully.

So down, down, down with hundreds of their families!

So falling, their people will go.

So down, down, down their leader will go.

"Twenty deaths were reported among our people, including Lady Rita, in the month after that. Now we try to avoid the earthkeepers at all cost. They always want their revenge until they are even with us."

"So *we* don't have the cleanest track record, either," I noted. I had always thought the light rune casters would never hurt an innocent society like that.

"Sometimes, to create peace, you must have a war," Marissa said. She surveyed the beach. "We can't go back to the human world. If we open another portal, the dark rune casters will know we're still on the mission." The earthkeepers had left, but I knew they couldn't have gone that far. "We'll drive along the beach for as long as we can," Marissa planned. "Then we'll go through the forest."

"What if the earthkeepers come back?" Kiara worried.

"Then we'll be careful," Jeremy answered.

We started to drive on the beach when the car stopped. I looked up at the car's dashboard. "It's out of gas," I explained. Marissa leaned back and hit her hands against the steering wheel.

"Can't you just magically make gas?" Kiara suggested.

"Magic doesn't work like that," Marissa said. "I can make gases but not car gas."

"Then why don't we just cast ethanol fuel, petroleum, hydrocarbons, and preservatives? These are what make up gas," Jeremy suggested.

Marissa looked at us all, unwilling to agree to his idea even though she knew it was right. Eventually, she sighed and then agreed. "Fine, I'll cast those into the gas tank."

We all got out of the car. I flipped open the gas tank and watched as Marissa cast each thing. I was amazed as I watched the liquids and gases forming as bubbles between her two hands and traveling into the gas tank without falling. All the science classes that had told me this was impossible just confused me when I could see the magic defying almost every law of physics out there.

Marissa looked up to her right. "Everyone get in the car!" she yelled, alarmed.

"Oh, what now?" Jeremy complained.

"Get in the car!" Marissa yelled again. We all ran into the car, shutting and locking our doors, and Marissa began to drive. She stepped hard on the gas pedal, making us all lurch back. I looked behind us to see what was upsetting Marissa so much and saw a gigantic gray storm cloud moving quickly in the sky above the beach.

"What is *that*?" I worried, causing Kiara and Jeremy to look back.

Kiara's eyes went wide. "It's a spell cloud. They're extremely hard to cast, and each storm cloud has a different thing coming out of it," she explained.

"Is it one of Twila's spells?" I asked.

"Let's hope not, because if it is, she knows we're still on the mission," Kiara replied. I gulped and looked forward, trying not to worry myself.

Jeremy pulled out a grey pen and pointed it at the cloud and the car. "According to my *verskag*, the cloud is only going two miles per hour and our car is going fifty miles per hour," he said. When I looked confused, he explained, "A *verskag* is a magical pen that can do many basic things. I got it for my birthday."

"Great thing his mom is filthy rich so she could buy it for him," Kiara muttered.

"For your information, my family is not filthy!" Jeremy fired back.

Kiara leaned away from him.

"We have bigger problems!" Marissa said, worrying us. "This car doesn't have enough gas to last for as long as the spell cloud will follow us. The spell cloud will also speed up gradually, so we will have to move quickly somehow."

I hoped whatever was hidden in the storm was not too vicious. As we were driving, I got a glimpse of something beginning to come out of the cloud, and it scared me to death. Wolves were falling out of the cloud. The wolves were landing on their feet and running, but only as far as the storm cloud reached.

"Wolves," I whimpered.

"What?" Kiara asked.

"Wolves are coming out of the storm cloud and they were sent by Twila," I said. "She knew that when I was little, I was scared of wolves. I had nightmares about them ever since she read me *Little Red Riding Hood*."

"What do we do if the wolves catch up?" Jeremy asked.

Kiara reached into the bag and began to pull out metal poles. Marissa explained, "I had the compound send these to us just in case we found ourselves in physical combat along the way." She threw each of us one of the staffs.

"When they catch up, we should stay in the car for protection, so we will open our windows," Marissa said. "I'm going to go out and refill the gas tank now while the cloud is still some distance away." We waited in silence as Marissa filled the tank. I didn't know if we could take on a pack of wolves. The rain of wolves had stopped, but the wolves on the ground were still there.

As Marissa got back in the car, I got an idea and told everyone. "Since the pack of wolves will stop when the cloud is gone, why don't we just make the cloud disappear?"

Jeremy contradicted my idea. "Magic doesn't work like that. You can't just make the cloud disappear. We have to do something that will cause the cloud to disappear."

"Like what?" I asked and then heard growls. We all looked behind the car to see the wolves arriving, running at full speed. Marissa immediately accelerated the car, and Jeremy tried to yell a plan to us above all the noise.

"If we all work together, we can freeze all the water in the cloud together. The ice will then fall, and the cloud will disappear. With no water, a cloud is just gas."

"Wow, Jeremy's actually smart. I didn't think that was possible," Kiara joked. I watched as the wolves came running toward us, and in my mind, it seemed like all the years I spent living with Twila blurred together. The woman who would tuck me in at night, care for me, tell me stories, congratulate me, and cheer me on could not have sent wolves to try to kill me. Their sharp fangs did not resemble the soft cloth of her turban that would touch me at night when she kissed me on the forehead. Twila was too caring to ever kill someone—but she had killed many people, and I had to accept that. But still, at that moment, I knew I could not kill her. To kill her would be evil.

Chapter 12 - The Wolves Arrive

My thoughts of Twila slipped away as the fear of the wolves took over my mind. I didn't know if I could defend myself. I had gone over twenty-four hours without any sleep and felt like I wanted to collapse. The wolves were close enough for me to see the drool coming out of their mouths from their hunger. They had their eyes on their dinner—and they were looking at us! I could tell that Kiara was even more scared than I was by her constant backward glimpses at the wolves; each time, her face would go pale when she saw them. Marissa was gripping the steering wheel so tight that her knuckles were turning white. Jeremy was holding the staff with an aggressive look on his face, ready for the wolves. I was just trying not to look back at the animals. Then I heard growling through my left ear. I knew what was outside my window but looked anyway. The first wolf to reach us was staring me right in the eye with a hungry look on its face.

"They're here," I whimpered. I looked at Marissa and she nodded, urging me to open the window. I did and the wolf took a leap for the window while running with the car. I smacked the wolf on its head with my staff when it was in the air. It fell to the ground and disappeared. I was proud until I saw Jeremy, who had whacked five wolves already. I whacked another one, but it seemed like they were just piling up next to my window.

"When should we cast the spell?" I yelled.

"Roll up your windows!" Marissa ordered. I rolled up my window, and when it was closed, the wolves began to bang against it. They were so close that their breath was fogging up the glass.

"Our minds need to think the same thing," Marissa explained. "Imagine that you're in the cloud, and all the water just forms together in a freezing ball." I tried to think, but my eyes could see that my window was beginning to crack every times the wolves struck their paws on it. I thought of the spell harder willing it to go quicker. I saw the storm cloud beginning to turn white. The spell wasn't working fast enough. The wolves hit the window again and it shattered. I could see a wolf reaching toward me, its paw inches away from my face. I never thought that this was how it would end! I closed my eyes and covered my head.

Nothing happened. I opened one eye to see that the wolf was gone. In fact, all of the wolves were gone, and the window was back together. Everyone around me was panting, looking relieved. I wondered if this was a dream, since the window was back together— or maybe I was dead.

"Where am I?" I asked aloud.

"The spell worked. I can't believe it, the spell worked!" Kiara cheered.

"Then how come the window is not shattered?" I asked.

"Because all living things made purely by magic effects disappear once they die or cease to exist," Jeremy said. "Duh, it's one of the basic laws of magic." *Like science, there are laws of magic, too,* I thought. Maybe the magic world wasn't so different after all.

"We should probably go to sleep in the car," Marissa suggested. "We can all recline our seats and sleep."

"Thank goodness, I'm exhausted!" Kiara said while reclining her seat. I reclined mine and the last thing I thought of before I fell asleep was Twila.

Chapter 13 - Curiosity Killed the Cat

When I woke up, I touched my hand to my hair and realized I hadn't brushed my hair or changed clothing in days. I grabbed my brush and a new set of clothes from my backpack. I pulled out my ponytail and put the hairband around my wrist. As I brushed my hair, Marissa, Kiara, and Jeremy continued to sleep. The car clock said it was already eleven in the morning; I should probably wake them soon.

My hair took about fifteen minutes to brush, it was so tangled. I went to the very back of the car where no one was sleeping. Since I wouldn't be going back to the human world, the clothes I had pulled out of the bag were rune caster clothes. There was a white T-shirt and underwear, black pants that were similar to yoga pants in the real world, and a black hoodie. I slipped on the clothes behind the seats so no one would see me if they woke up.

Once I changed, I went back to my seat. My backpack was open, so I spotted the phone I had received for the mission. Twila had a phone like this, so I knew how to use it. The phone in my hands was a little piece of the human world that comforted me. It made me feel like I was back in the human world.

I saw an app I had never seen before that had been downloaded onto my phone. It had a picture of a cartoon pink heart with a white background. The title of the app was in Japanese, so I couldn't read it. Led by curiosity, I opened the app. Immediately, a bunch of code began to take up the whole screen. It was scrolling through quickly, even though I wasn't touching the screen. Scared, I shook Marissa awake. "Marissa!" I yelled.

She opened her eyes with a groggy look on her face, but immediately her eyes went wide when she saw the phone. She snatched it out of my hand so quickly that the buttons left a scratch on my hand. She unlocked the car and flung open the door. Still with the phone in her hand, she ran toward the water as fast as she could. Without hesitating, she chucked the phone into the water. I opened up my door and jogged to her, sand grains filling my shoes. "What was that for?" I exclaimed.

"I'll answer that as soon as you answer this. What did you do on that phone this morning?" she demanded. I began to worry—she was acting as if what I did with the phone could jeopardize the mission.

I told Marissa about the app. "Everyone was asleep, so I decided to check out the phone. There was an app that I thought might be useful, and I was curious, so I opened it. Then all of a sudden, all this code went scrolling through the phone."

Marissa shook her head. "That code was tracking you. Anything else you do on that phone besides texting us is not safe. There are tech geniuses with the dark rune casters that can hack into the phone. We have to drive as far away from that phone as possible now. The dark rune casters will get to that phone as fast as they can because they think it's with you. Now get back in the car."

I headed back to the car and sat down in the seat with the door still open to dump the sand out of the sneakers I had put on this morning. Once the sneakers were empty, I slipped them back on and closed my door. Marissa locked the car and put the key in the ignition. We started going at a steady pace.

Jeremy slowly opened his eyes and yawned. "What time is it?" he said quietly, barely awake.

"Past twelve," I answered. His hair was messed up and his shirt had dirt all over the side. His shoes were muddy on the bottom and coated in sand. I realized that we hadn't walked out in the sand, but Jeremy's shoes were covered in it. I wondered when he had gone out and what he had been doing. I hadn't noticed it before, but he was also more tired and messy than the rest of us, and that was saying something.

"When did you go out on the beach?" I asked pointing at his shoes.

He looked at me and then looked out the window. He always tried to hide his feelings and act like nothing was wrong, but I could see the reflection of his worried face in the window. What was he so scared of me finding out?

I watched Marissa. After everything that had happened on this mission, I could tell she wanted to take things into her own hands. She was now driving, not using a spell to drive. Or was it just that the rune casting world was a lot more dangerous than the human world?

I still wasn't prepared for my encounter with Twila, physically or mentally. I had taken a few karate classes as a kid, but I couldn't take down an evil rune caster with that little bit of training. We had overcome many challenges on this mission, but in the end, the only challenge that mattered was at the dark rune casters' lair. That was the challenge we were least prepared for.

"Just a few more days until we arrive," Marissa said. "Once we get far away enough from the phone, we need to stop for training."

Jeremy looked confused and turned toward Marissa. "What do you mean, *get away from the phone*?" he asked.

I admitted my mistake. "I opened an app on my phone that let someone begin to track it, so Marissa threw it into the water."

Jeremy seemed stunned. "You did what? What were you thinking, Emma? Now they're on our trail. In fact, they're probably following us right now. You might've destroyed our chances of succeeding at this mission and living to tell about it!"

"It was a mistake! I didn't know any better," I answered. He gave me a dirty look and then returned to staring out the window.

"What's all the shouting about?" Kiara groaned, awakening.

"A mistake," I replied, glaring at Jeremy. Kiara looked at us, confused, but then just shook her head.

"Why, Jeremy, do you have to be so judgmental all the time?" Kiara said.

"Because people are always doing things wrong," he said.

"Why don't you just give people a chance to show you they're not wrong?" Kiara suggested. Jeremy didn't say anything back and seemed to be considering a different idea than his own, for once.

Kiara nodded at me, happy to see she had made progress with an impossible subject. Then her phone began to ring. I was curious to see who was calling; it was probably just someone who had the wrong number. She picked up her phone and looked at it.

"Emma, why are you calling me?" she asked. My stomach dropped, but I couldn't speak fast enough, and she answered the phone. We all stared at her with petrified faces. She had been asleep and didn't hear our conversation about the phone.

"Thank you for leaving the phone for us and leading us right to you. Expect your mission to end a little quicker than you thought!" a male voice on the other line snickered. Kiara hung up and was now wearing the scared look we all had when she answered the phone.

"It sunk to the bottom of the ocean. I should've known they could retrieve that phone," Marissa complained. Kiara didn't need to ask any questions about what happened. She knew that the dark rune casters had found the phone, and that was enough.

"Everyone, give me your phones right now," Marissa commanded. She grabbed the phones out of our hands and took her own out of her bag. She ran out onto the beach and chucked them in the opposite direction from where we were going. She came back into the car looking frantic.

"I'm going to write a message explaining what happened to Ebonhaunt and send it through my transmitter," she planned aloud.

"I'll ask for aircraft and backup in the message." She took out a pen and paper from her bag and began to write as fast a she could. "Oops, I forgot," she said absently. She waved her hand, and the car began to drive. I wondered if the dark rune casters would get to us before the backup came, but we could only wait and prepare for the worst. Worried thoughts about what would happen next ran through my mind: *What if they kill us? Is this my last day? What have I gotten myself into? If only I hadn't opened that app!* Everyone else's faces had filled with the most worry I had ever seen on them before. We all knew what would happen if the dark rune casters got to us before our allies. I didn't even realize that we were driving super fast until I saw the scenery blurring outside my window. We began to drive up a hill from the beach into a forest.

"This is a longer way, but it will get the dark rune casters off our track for a little bit. I sent the message and Ebonhaunt replied, saying they are coming as fast as they can. That stupid signal was finally working," Marissa said, putting my mind slightly at ease.

"Won't the dark rune casters be able to track aircraft easily?" I asked.

"They are already hot on our trail, so why not move a little faster in the air?" Marissa replied. I couldn't wait for that plane to come; it would make me feel safer, not abandoned in the wilderness with no defense. We needed help, and it needed to come soon. I hoped we would live through another day. I had just discovered this world, and I didn't want to leave it just yet. Our faces grew less worried than before; now we had hope. Hope was an amazing thing to have at a time like this. The car was still driving, though, and until we got into that plane, we weren't safe.

"Where are we?" I asked.

"The Sacred Forest," Marissa answered.

"Isn't this where the earthkeepers live?" I asked. "Isn't it dangerous?"

"The earthkeepers were moved out of the Sacred Forest a long time ago. No evil is to reside in here. It is the halfway mark between the dark rune casting lair and Ebonhaunt. The only peaceful moments between dark rune casters and light rune casters have happened here. We share the clear water running through the streams here but we don't try to drown each other. We both pray here but not for harm to come to one another. We discuss peace treaties and land here but don't trick each other. Of course, only the nicest of the dark rune casters will come here—only the ones who regret killing," Marissa explained.

"Has every dark rune caster killed someone?" I asked.

Marissa replied, "Every dark rune caster must kill one of their family members to join the dark rune casters. It is a horrible thing that we don't like to talk about. But the Sacred Forest can let you pray to the dead. Some dark rune casters pray for their victims' forgiveness. If a ghost would like, it may appear and listen only if someone is praying for it here. To pray here, you must give your reason to the guards of the prayer circle. If you are an important person or have a good reason, you are allowed to pray. But you must be very careful with your wording when you pray here, because if

74

the spirits agree to help you, they will do exactly what your prayer says. So if you pray for someone to fall in love with you, he might fall in love with some random person if you do not specify who *you* is. There have been tragic incidents."

"Is that why the Sacred Forest is so sacred?" I asked.

Kiara answered me this time, "Yes."

My mind was still filled with curiosity, so I asked another question. "What makes the prayer circle so magical?"

"All the trees in this forest are magical," Kiara told me. "It's the only forest this big with all magical trees. When you put all that pure magic together, there are amazing effects. The prayer circle is an effect of the magical trees."

"But what's so magical about the trees?" I asked. "They seem just like regular trees."

"Look up," Jeremy said. I looked up out of my window to see some trees filled with weirdly colored and shaped fruits. One tree was covered in purple squares, and another one was growing black triangles. Other trees had branches that bended together into weird shapes. One tree's branches looked liked they had formed into a hanging house. After we drove farther, I saw a few more branch houses. I was amazed when I saw that two raccoons were sleeping in one of the branch houses. Even the animals that I was familiar with acted differently in this world, and they didn't scatter when our car came by.

There were a lot of scary things in this world, but there were a lot of beautiful things, too. I was sitting in wonder of magic while people were hunting me down. This world was so confusing! I just tried to do what everyone else was doing to make it easier to understand. I still was sort of expecting to wake up from a dream. This probably was just a dream—it just seemed longer than a dream from one night's sleep. Twila would wake me up any moment and tell me that it was time to go to work. But if it was a dream, why did I get tired and go to bed, or cry?

I didn't want some of it to be a dream—like the amazing friends I had made or my parents. If I woke up from this dream, I would still never forget this world. But Twila was not who she was before—in this dream or in this life. In this life, she no longer cared for me. She wouldn't help me up if I fell or hurt myself....

All of a sudden, we heard plane noises above us.

"There it is!" Marissa exclaimed. "It won't be able to land here, so we'll have to drive out of the forest over there." She pointed to our left, where there was an empty field that looked big enough for a plane.

We turned around and drove to the field, trying to avoid the trees. We parked the car and watched as the plane landed. The plane was huge and looked fancier than a private jet. Once the plane landed, we got out of the car. The back of the plane opened, and a man walked out toward us. He was wearing black dressy plants and a long black trench coat. He had on shades. The plane was making a lot of air blow around, so his black hair flapped in the wind. He looked about Colonel James's age.

"Good day, Marissa, is this her?" the man asked in a German accent, pointing to me. Marissa nodded her head. "It is an honor to meet you Ms. Westley. My name is Warren Clarke."

The man reached out his hand for me to shake. I did so and greeted him, "It's nice to meet you, Mr. Clarke."

He clapped his hand over mine and laughed, "Oh, please call me Warren."

"Warren is an officer at Ebonhaunt. He is a descendant of a Deliverer from many generations ago." Marissa introduced him like he was highly esteemed at Ebonhaunt.

"Thank you, Marissa, for the kind introduction, but we must get going." Warren hurried us toward the plane that was waiting for us. "Now, be careful I don't want this baby to get scratched up. It's newly built with defensive capabilities, guns, twenty-seven rooms, and a bulletproof exterior. Oh, and it has a training room for all your needs." he explained.

This was cooler than any airplane I'd ever seen! The door in the back had foldout stairs. We stepped into the first room, where there was a table filled with drinks and sweets. There was another table in the center with plane seats surrounding it.

"Shall I give you a tour?" Warren offered. Marissa nodded her head. "This is one of the main living areas where passengers can hang out and enjoy meals." He gestured to the room, then led us out to the hallway, where there were ten doors. Each door had a white board with one of our names on it. "These are your bedrooms that you will be staying in for the next couple of days. Each room has a bathroom for your sanitary needs. Here is a map for each of you so that you may explore the rest of the plane later on." He handed us each a map. "If you would please follow me, I would like to introduce you to someone."

Warren led us back through the main living area and into the cockpit at the front of the plane. There was a woman with a headset and her hands on the controls. She had thick, black, bouncy hair and looked about the same age as Warren.

"This is my wife, Linda," Warren introduced us.

Linda shook Marissa's, Kiara's, and Jeremy's hands, smiling. But when she got to me, she cupped her hand over her mouth and turned to Warren. She brought her hand down and asked, "Is this her?"

Warren nodded his head, looking proud to have "brought" me to her She grabbed both my hands and looked at me with a happy face.

"It is *so* nice to finally meet you!" She dragged out her words, amazed. I was unsure of what to say. She seemed so happy that I didn't want to disappoint her with who I really was.

"It's really nice to meet you, too," I stuttered. I wondered why these people were so excited to meet me—they seemed much more excited than everyone else.

"You're such a beautiful girl," Linda gushed. "I am so lucky to have you in the Deliverer family."

I was shocked. "Deliverer family?" I asked.

"You didn't know? All the Deliverers and anyone related to them by blood are in the Deliverer's family," Linda explained. "It is separate from your biological family."

I couldn't believe these people were my family—and that I had two families! There were so many different secrets of the rune casting world that I learned at least one new thing every day!

"Wow, hi," I said, stunned.

Linda giggled and apologized. "I'm sorry, I didn't mean to be a complete stranger oohing and ahhing over you. I know it must be awkward. There are just no children in our family, so you are almost like a niece to us."

"It's okay," I said. "I barely have any family, so it would be really nice to have a new aunt and uncle."

"Well, we have to get back to work, but why don't you all go hang out in the plane?" Linda said.

I headed off with everyone else. They all sat down around the table in the living area.

"Emma, aren't you going to come hang out?" Kiara asked.

"I'm actually going to go to my bedroom," I said.

"Okay." Kiara turned back around to face everyone else. I opened my bedroom door and flopped down onto the queen-sized bed. It was the first bed I had been on in days.

I grabbed a pillow and began to cry. I just wasn't ready to replace Twila as my aunt. Twila had practically been my mother for my whole life. I would love to have another aunt and uncle, but not quite yet.

I might not be alive if it weren't for Twila, so how could I kill her? There had to be some way I could keep her from hurting anyone but not kill her. Twila was too strong for any imprisonment. I hoped that I could figure something out in the moment and negotiate with her. She wouldn't hurt me, I knew that, because those wolves could've been bigger and stronger if she had wanted them to be. She had been given many opportunities, but she hadn't taken them. Maybe she just wanted something from me—but she could've easily captured us.

How could she be so evil? No matter how many times I tried to find an explanation for Twila, I found nothing. I realized that she must never have been truly kind to me—it was all an act to her. But she could've killed me because she knew that I was destined to kill her. She wanted to keep me away from this world—never to meet my parents, meet new friends, or discover all the amazing secrets about rune casting. Twila had been lying to me my whole life, so she must be evil.

I went into the bathroom and wiped my tears. I used a tissue to make it look like I hadn't been crying. Then I realized that I hadn't taken a shower in days. I made sure there was soap and shampoo in the shower.

After my shower, I got back into the clothes I had been wearing before and began to comb out my hair in front of the sink. It was so nice to be in an actual bathroom for once on the mission. Almost everything in the bathroom was made out of marble, and brushes, combs, toothbrushes, and soap were provided. Then I realized that there was no blow dryer to dry my hair.

I reached for a towel but then realized that I could try magic to dry my hair. I concentrated, thinking of the hot air blowing out of a blow dryer, and hot air began to blow out of my hand. I hovered my hands over my hair and it dried. I was proud—magic was getting easier and easier each day. I was going to try to use magic more often!

I walked over to my bed and picked up the map that Warren had given me. I found the training room on the paper. I walked out of my room and down the hall, turning left and down another hall.

I finally opened a steel door, and inside was the training room. It was gigantic—the whole floor was covered in mats. In one corner was a gigantic glass box with a door that about ten people could fit in. Above the door was a sign that read *Magic Simulator.*

Another wall was lined with all the weapons you could think of—aside from guns. There were swords, spears, bows and arrows, metal nun-chucks, and poles with spiky ends. Another area contained many metal and plush hanging punching bags—there was knuckle tape on a table, as well. Next to that area there were targets. There was a pull-up bar hanging on the wall and two white marks stretched across the floor with a timer on the wall.

I headed over to the punching bags. I needed to strengthen myself quickly, because I was rather weak at the moment. I wrapped my knuckles in the tape and stood in front of a red plush punching bag hanging by chains. I began to punch it, causing the bag to move a tiny bit, and repeated a pattern in my head: *1, 2, pause, 1, 2, pause.* Sweat began to roll down my head, so I went to a cart in the room and grabbed a bottle of water off of it. I sat down and drank the entire bottle.

I already knew where I was going next: the magic simulator. I walked over to it and looked at a touch screen on the machine that read: *Please enter your skill level: beginner, intermediate, or advanced.* I clicked the beginner button. The machine conveyed another message: *Please step into the glass case with nothing except yourself. If at any time you would like to end the challenge before you have completed it, yell, "Red alert."* I stepped into the glass case and closed the door behind me. A digital woman with a tight blonde bun appeared and began to talk.

"In this challenge, black birds will try to attack you. You must destroy all the birds before the clock ends. When you are ready to begin, press the green button to your left."

First, I decided on what to use against the birds that I already knew how to cast. I decided on fire. I pressed the green button and a blackbird appeared, flying straight toward me. I burned it with fire, and then another one appeared. I burned this one, too. Once I burned a bird, it disappeared. Then more and more appeared, and I couldn't hit them all. More and more of their beaks made contact with my skin, sending searing pains over my body.

"Stop." I yelled. "Red alert!"

The blackbirds disappeared and the machine spoke. "Mission failed."

I was still sitting alone in the glass case. I lay down, panting. Even though I knew the birds weren't real, they still caused me pain. But the marks I thought were on me from the birds hitting me in the simulation were gone and the pain had disappeared. I stood up, opened the glass door, and walked out. I didn't realize how tired I was until then. There was sweat rolling down my face, and I flopped down on the floor without thinking. I spread out on the ground and put my hands on my chest. I stood up once I caught my breath and saw that Marissa, Kiara, and Jeremy had walked into the room.

"We need to do some combat training," Marissa said. I went over to the weapons rack and picked up a sword. Kiara and Jeremy did, too, and we all stood in a line while Marissa taught us techniques.

"Emma, would you walk over with me to the magic simulator?" I walked with Marissa to the glass case. She pressed a few buttons and then explained what she did. "I adjusted the magic simulator so it will give you combat training. Wolves are going to appear, and you must hit them with your sword."

I walked into the magic simulator with my sword and pressed the green button. Wolves began to appear, and I hit each one with the weapon, spinning and changing hands. Some wolves ran at me, and some wolves came from above, but I didn't let a single one touch me. When they all were gone, the machine said, "Mission complete."

Feeling proud, I put down my sword and opened the door of the glass case.

"Great job," Marissa praised me. Jeremy and Kiara were sitting down now without their swords.

"We should walk back to the main living area," Marissa said. "Warren would like to meet with us about our plan." We all walked with her out the door and down the hallway. In the main living area, Warren was already sitting at the table waiting for us. We all sat down.

"Strap in, it might get bumpy," Warren said. I strapped my seatbelt on. It was just like a regular plane's seatbelt.

He continued, "We are predicting that it will take about one day to get to the dark rune casters' lair. But we will have to land early and drive in one of our mission cars so they do not see the plane. We will be entering through secret tunnels, but I will not be going in with you, because I have not been approved by Ebonhaunt to do so. Marissa and Kiara will go find the captured and bring them to the secret tunnels, where I will meet them and escort them to the plane. Meanwhile, Emma and Jeremy will go after Twila. Once Emma and Jeremy are done, they will meet Marissa and Kiara at the tunnels, but if they aren't there, Emma and Jeremy should go to the plane. Marissa and Kiara will also go to the plane if something happens. You will be given a full map and more detailed plan closer to the mission's time."

"Can I share my worry?" I asked and Warren nodded his head. "Twila is one of the most powerful rune casters in the whole world and has been performing magic for years. I have just started my training and barely know anything about this world. How will I defeat her? It's simply not possible."

Kiara was playing with her hands; I could tell she was bored. Warren answered me, "Ebonhaunt is working on a very special tool for you to do so."

Kiara looked up and put her hands at rest. "What kind of tool?" she asked.

"That's classified until it's ready. But I can tell you, its quite amazing," Warren bragged. I was excited to see what my new tool would be, but for now, I would have to wait.

"What will I do to help on the mission?" Jeremy asked.

"You'll lead Emma to the room where Twila will be and hide outside," Warren explained. "Only come in if Emma says the word *nickel*. That's when you'll come in and help Emma if she needs it."

All of a sudden sirens began to go off.

"They found us, and they're close!" Warren panicked. I began to feel a pit growing in my stomach. I was scared. We heard a sound like hard rain was falling on the plane.

Warren steadied himself and looked grim. "They're trying to hit us with bullets, but the plane is bulletproof. We need to prepare for any other tricks they have up their sleeves!"

Linda rushed in. "You paged me, Warren? I put Cameron in charge of flying for now, since he's done fighting in planes before."

"Good. I paged you because I wanted to make sure you were safe. Now, go tell Cameron that when he sees red lights flashing, they have managed to board the plane. He should then put the plane on autopilot," Warren ordered. Linda nodded her head and hurried out.

"Everyone else, go to the training room and grab some weapons for yourselves," Warren commanded. We all rushed to the training room. At every step, it seemed like the pit in my stomach was growing bigger and bigger. I was scared that the dark rune casters would get us this time, and the only people in the world I cared deeply about would die: my family, my friends, and my mentors. All of Ebonhaunt would then be hanging by a thread, and I didn't know if the community would be able to survive without a leader guiding them. I was scared for everyone, and I could tell that my teammates were, too.

We opened the door to the training room and shuffled through nervously. Everyone else was grabbing two weapons, so I grabbed two swords. Just in case something happened, I grabbed a sheathed dagger on the wall and slipped it into my boot outside of the sock. I kept the blade cased. We all ran out of the room carrying the weapons and not speaking to each other. We came back into the main living area, where Linda and Warren were already standing and talking with another member of the plane's crew. We put the extra weapons on a chair and kept the rest in our hands.

Warren looked at his pager. "Shoot! Linda, go show them the emergency room. I'll go get Cameron and the others." He kissed her on the head and ran off toward the cockpit.

Linda began to hurry in the other direction. "Everyone, follow me," she said. It looked like we were headed to the training room, but I was surprised when we passed it. Linda took a key from her belt and opened a big metal door. We walked in to find out it was not a room but another plane. There were many controls at the front and lots of nice leather seats in the back with a table, a fridge, and some crates of supplies.

"We will be flying this plane to the dark compound, because the dark rune casters have almost managed to enter the main plane. If we were to stop them at this point, we would risk a part of the main plane malfunctioning," Linda told us. "Cameron is putting the plane in the right position so we can leave."

I hadn't even met the other crew members, but I hoped Warren and they were safe. I watched as Linda began to power the plane up. "Come on, Warren," she muttered as the red flashing lights began to go off, meaning the dark rune casters had made it inside.

Warren and three other members of the flight crew burst through the metal door to the plane and slammed it shut. "Let's get flying quickly," he ordered. I could hear voices in the hallway while Linda was madly moving switches and pressing buttons. The voices were getting closer and closer. I could tell Warren noticed it, too, because he walked over to the door and put ice around it, making it a difficult job for the dark rune casters to open it unless they knew the ice was there.

Jeremy, Kiara, and I had barely said anything this whole time because we were so scared. I wondered why Marissa, Linda, and Warren weren't as scared—probably because they had been through much worse. Warren walked over to Linda and sat down in the other pilot seat next to her and they began to talk together. Cameron walked over to the only other seat—next to me, to my left. The seats were arranged in pairs, so he was the only person sitting next to me. I was surprised that they let Cameron pilot the plane; he looked only about my age. He was shaking, squeezing his hands together. I could tell he had never been in a situation like this before; after all, I never thought *I* would be, especially at this age.

I reached out my hand for him to shake. "I'm Emma," I introduced myself.

He shook it. "Cameron," he said. He smiled. It seemed like he was friendly, but from how he reacted to me introducing myself, it also seemed like he hadn't been shown much hospitality before. He was one of the most handsome boys I had seen in this world. I wasn't into him or anything—it was just something I noticed. He had brownish-orange hair that was cut just right to outline his face but didn't grow past his ears. He had piercing blue eyes that reminded me of the ocean and soft plump lips. Cameron had a perfect face. But this was no time to think about boys, people's lives were at stake! I decided that I had to have a friendly conversation though, because I hadn't had one that didn't involve rune casting plans in ages.

"You're pretty young to be flying, aren't you?" I asked.

"Yah, I'm one of the youngest pilots," he answered, "But I've been obsessed with planes ever since I was little—the way they can soar up into the sky and you can just forget everything else 'cause it's all below you. I don't like this type of flying. I just want to fly for fun, because here, the problems stay with the plane—they don't just stay on the ground. I would enjoy this more if there wasn't always someone ordering me around. I just want to fly." He paused. "I'm sorry, I just really needed to get that out," he apologized.

"No, no, it's okay. I love hearing people's opinions. And to be honest, I haven't had much of a regular conversation in this world 'til today," I admitted.

"I've always wanted to see the human world," Cameron said. "We're just not allowed to. I feel like I don't have any freedom sometimes." He really was nice and just wanted to see the world— that is, both worlds.

"I'm not sure I can keep up with this whole Deliverer thing," I blurted. "They just expect so much from me when I sometimes don't even believe this is real. How am I supposed to kill the most powerful dark rune caster? They act like it's so easy to just kill the person who raised you your whole life, but I'm actually extremely nervous." I realized I was crying now. I guess I, too, had just really needed to get that out.

"It's okay, I understand," Cameron said. "I think you'll figure things out. From what I know about you so far, you're nice, smart, caring, considerate, and courageous. You'll do fine." When he put his hand on my knee and gave me an encouraging look, I could feel the blood rush to my cheeks. I turned away so he wouldn't see. He was so nice! I looked back at him, smiling.

"Thank you for that, and thank you for understanding," I said. He smiled back at me. We stared at each other for about twenty seconds and then snapped out of it. It was crazy how we had come to empathize with each other so quickly. But I couldn't have a crush on him! I mean, I didn't know him. My stomach filled with butterflies when he smiled at me.

Then Warren yelled, "They found us!"

What was I thinking? I didn't have time for a love life. I was too busy being chased by dark rune casters.

Chapter 14 - The Battle Begins

"The dark rune casters are about thirty feet below us," Warren informed Linda.

"Below us? Oh, no, if they hit us enough from the bottom of the plane, we're going to have a big problem," Linda replied. I wished they were whispering, because now I was shaking with fear. This time we might not be so lucky as before. The plane began to speed up—it tilted upward and then continued straight forward. I looked through my window and saw a duplicate of our plane emerge out of the clouds. They were using our plane!

"Warren, they're using the same kind of plane as this one," I nervously told him.

He put his hand to his forehead and groaned, "Oh, shoot, we don't have a chance. This plane has the best protective and attack system that any plane has ever had."

I felt a bump underneath us, and the whole plane shook. "Warren, they've made contact!" Linda said. Something hit us underneath again and this time the plane shook even more.

I could see Warren and Linda madly work the steering and controls. The plane shot downward, so the next time, it was hit in the back. Another hit scored on the wing, and I watched as part of the wing broke off. The plane began to drop rapidly. Warren and Linda somehow made the plane slow and descend less steeply.

I wondered if this would be how I'd die—in a plane crash. I had just met my parents and someone whom I thought I could really care for, and now I was about to die. Wow, the world really did hate me.

We were getting closer and closer to the ground. Cameron grabbed my hand and squeezed. We held our hands together to our faces, preparing for impact. I opened my eyes, looking through Cameron's hands as the plane slid on the ground, breaking trees, and rolled to one side. I felt like I might puke.

The plane rolled on the side where Marissa and Kiara were sitting. Marissa was closest to the window. The two windows on that side shattered, and pieces rained down on them. Luckily, the plane wasn't totally on its side. The plane rolled a little again and part of the window next to me broke, little pieces of shattered glass flying in the air. Cameron and I held our arms to our faces. I leaned over on to him and he leaned even farther to his side. I felt a piece of glass slice my arm, and I squealed. Everything felt like it was going in slow motion, and so much was happening that I barely noticed the shard of glass. I realized I was crying again. Was I going to die?

"It's over," Cameron said, moving my arms away from my face. I whimpered, and he held my face in his hands. "It's okay, it's all over. But we have to get out of here." I opened my eyes. The plane was now perfectly flat on the ground. I unbuckled and stood up. Cameron unbuckled and put his hand behind my back. Everything was a blur—I didn't know what was going on.

Cameron opened an exit door. He lifted me, put me outside, and jumped out, too. We walked far away from the plane, and I crouched down. He looked like he was in shock also.

"I don't think I'm ever going to love flying as much as I used to," Cameron said. I nodded, agreeing. I saw Jeremy stumble out of the plane, followed by Warren and Linda. Cameron sat down on the ground, and Warren and Linda came over to us. Jeremy saw us and walked over.

"Where are Kiara and Marissa?" Linda asked, and I felt like I had been punched in the stomach. I hurried away from everyone else and puked. Oh, my gosh, I couldn't believe I just did that in front of Cameron and everyone else! But I felt much better afterward. Cameron handed me a handkerchief from his pocket, and I wiped my mouth.

Just then, Kiara hopped out of the plane with a sad look on her face and tears rolling down her cheeks. She casted a spell making a body float through the air only this body wasn't moving. Immediately, I knew who it was, and my heart began to pound. Kiara dropped the body on the ground and stared at us with a blank expression. I stood up, and Cameron walked with me, supporting me as I staggered over to Kiara and Marissa.

I looked down to see a pale woman with thin brown hair, neatly brushed, with tiny pieces of glass tangled in it and a nice leather jacket. Her blue eyes stared up at the sky, not blinking, and her lips looked as dry as a desert. A piece of glass was sticking out of her stomach. I covered my mouth and turned away, putting my head into Cameron's chest. He put his arms around my head and stroked my hair. I felt his warm breath on my head when he buried his face in my hair. That body was not the strong woman I knew—

the one full of laughter and jokes that sometimes didn't need to be heard. This woman lying before me was so pale that it seemed like her lively soul had just been sucked out of her. A body without a soul was just a body—no meaning, no purpose, it was just a body. I slipped out of Cameron's arms and saw Kiara still staring at Marissa in shock.

"She's dead," Kiara muttered. "They did this! How could you murder an innocent person?" Kiara began to yell.

"Kiara, the dark rune casters are evil. That's why we have to stop them," I said.

"I'm not talking about the dark rune casters," Kiara answered. "I'm talking about Ebonhaunt! They sent us on this mission knowing there was the chance that people would die. Maybe they just selected the people they hated in order to kill them!"

"No, Kiara," I said, "you know it's not like that. This is one of the most important missions in history. They wouldn't have sent people who were bad. Ebonhaunt is trying to protect everyone!"

Kiara motioned to Marissa. "Well, look how that turned out." She spun and walked away.

Ebonhaunt was trying to protect us, right? Sometimes, we just had to make sacrifices. I gulped, and Warren came over with a blanket. Linda waved her hand and a hole appeared dug in the ground. Warren wrapped Marissa in a blanket. He then dropped her into the hole. I waved my hand and dirt appeared on top of her. Then Kiara walked over with a piece of the plane in her hand and stuck it on top of the grave.

"Thank you for your help, guidance, and kindness," Linda said.

We stared at the grave in silence for a few minutes until Warren said, "I contacted Ebonhaunt, and we have all been given permission to join the mission. We should set up camp in the forest. But first we must walk for awhile—the dark rune casters will scout the area near the plane crash." Nobody replied. We all just followed him into the forest, leaving the grave and the plane behind.

As we walked through the trees, I stepped into something squishy. It looked and felt like a big puddle of black mud. Only one of my feet was in the puddle, and when I tried to lift it, my foot wouldn't come out.

Jeremy glanced back at me. "Don't move!" he yelled. Everyone looked in my direction, and I froze. I was right behind Warren, who was in the lead, but he hadn't stepped in this goo.

"You've stepped in a black sucker—and if you move, it will try to pull you under! Wait, what forest are we in?" Jeremy asked.

"I didn't want to scare you, but we crash-landed in the Gertred Forest," Warren said. Everyone else began to look worried. I was confused.

"What's the Gertred Forest?" I inquired.

"It's a forest named after one of the dark rune caster Deliverers, Warren informed me. "He grew this forest around the dark lair to protect it. This black sucker is one of the obstacles that you should fear the least but still watch out for. There are other things that live and move around this forest that you should be more afraid of. Here!" He grabbed a flask out of his backpack and poured water on my foot. I pulled out my foot with no trace of goo on it.

"Thanks."

We continued walking, but now I could tell that everyone was filled with fear. I could've guessed this was a dark forest, because the tree branches and leaves were mostly black and were so big that they blocked almost all light from getting to the forest floor. The only light came from little slivers of sun sneaking in through cracks in the tree branches' web. And the forest sounds were different than any other forest sounds I had ever heard. You could hear the occasional gust of wind going so fast that it made a howling noise. We could also hear some periodic growling and the crunch of twigs beneath our feet.

Since that first encounter, I had already avoided six of the black suckers. The only time anyone talked was when Warren gave us directions. I guess we were all scared that we would end up like Marissa. Cameron was now standing next to me, and I tried to match my footsteps to his to steady my heartbeat. It was an old trick I had learned back in seventh grade. I had used that trick a lot throughout my life when I was scared or felt like I was about to cry: when someone would make fun of me because I could never fit in, or when I got a bad grade because I usually got A's, or when I fell down and hurt myself. It always helped, and I was already feeling better.

Warren stopped in a clearing in the middle of the forest and said, "This might not be the safest place, but it's the only place. Let's make camp here, and I'll take the first watch."

Unlike other places in the forest, the branches weren't woven over us, and we had a clear view of the stars and moon. It was truly beautiful, for there were no city lights. I gazed at the sky until I was snapped out of it by a distant howl. I put my backpack on the ground and took out a blanket and pillow. It felt as if the minute I rested my head on the pillow, I fell asleep.

Chapter 15 - The Day

"Rise and shine! We've got a big day ahead of us!" Warren yelled, waking us.

I rubbed my eyes and sat up. I realized today was the day—the day I would have to kill Twila. I gulped, folded up my blanket, and put it in my backpack along with my pillow. Because the dark rune casters were pursuing us so closely, there was no way for Eberhaunt to send me the secret weapon. I was going to have to rely on whatever special talents a Deliverer is born with to fight Twila. I took my sword out from under my backpack and strapped it onto my belt. I watched as everyone nervously got up. Being this close to the Dark Lair, we were all so nervous, no one felt like talking. I stood up and slung on my backpack. We gathered around Warren.

"So, here's the new plan. Emma and Cameron will go after Twila using this path," he explained, handing me a parchment map with a red ink route drawn on it. "Jeremy, since we sadly do not have Marissa with us, you will now go with Linda, Kiara, and me to get the prisoners following this path." He held up another map. "Now, follow me. What you're about to see may be quite surprising."

We walked to the corner of the field, and Warren traced his hand around a part of the grass in a square formation. He grabbed onto a handle that appeared and pulled it up, revealing a stone set of stairs. Warren stepped down onto the stairs. The rest of us all stared, except Linda, who was already beginning to climb down.

"Well, what are you waiting for?" Warren urged. I stepped down onto the stone stairs, and a chill crept over me. Kiara, Cameron, Jeremy, and finally Warren followed. Down about fifteen stairs, I stepped into a square tunnel only big enough for two people to walk side by side and still be a little squished. There were rune shapes carved into the walls, and it would have been dark if Linda hadn't cast a ball of light into her hand.

"Sorry it's so cold. We haven't used this tunnel in at least a hundred years, and the people who built it thousands of years ago forgot to put in a heater," Warren joked.

We came to a fork in the tunnel, and Warren turned to face us. "Now, this is where we split up. We are now under the lair, so don't make a lot of noise. Good luck!"

Cameron and I turned left and went down a diagonal tunnel, following the map. As we walked, our footsteps echoed in the silence. The runes were different in this part of the tunnel; they all had squares in them. The other hallway had triangles in all the runes. We walked until we reached another set of spiral stone stairs. We glanced at each other.

"This is it," I whispered. "Wait down here. I'll yell *nickel* if I need you."

Cameron nodded. I slowly began to walk up the stairs. With every step, my mind raced more and more. I wasn't ready. I dropped my backpack under a trapdoor in the ceiling, which was low enough to reach. My heart pounded and I put my hands to the door. Hesitantly, I pushed it open and stepped out. I closed the door without making a sound, and then it blended into the ground as if there was no door. A woman sitting in a black chair had her back to me. I saw the turban, and I felt like I was going to faint. It was Twila. I slowly walked toward her quietly, with my sword in my hand.

"Did you really think you could sneak up on me?" Twila cackled, turning her chair around. I saw the necklace everyone had been talking about. It was a perfect, shiny emerald with a silver triangle carved into it. The pendant was hanging on a black chord.

"You look taller—have you grown? I'm so happy to finally see you," Twila said in a sarcastic voice. She truly looked devious. The evil smile on her face made her look like she had something very special planned for me. She took off her floral silk turban, and her brown wavy hair fell down onto her shoulders. I didn't answer. I was squeezing the sword hard because I was nervous. "What, is my conversation boring?" Twila laughed. She glanced at my sword. "Oh, you want to fight. Well, you do know what you're up against. What kind of evil person fights the one who took care of her for her whole life."

She stood and walked toward me. When she got close enough, I slashed her face with my sword. She held her hand to the cut on her cheek, revealing blood.

"It's not called evil, it's called sacrifice, for people's safety," I argued.

She looked surprised. "Ooh, feisty, but I can tell you haven't grown into Ebonhaunt's ways yet." She waved her hand, and a card appeared there. She handed it to me. It read *R.I.P. Colonel James. Please show your support by attending his funeral.* There was a black and white picture of Colonel James at the top.

"It was too bad I had to kill him. He was actually growing on me," Twila said as if it were nothing. "But sadly, that's what happens when you don't follow my rules."

I charged at her with my sword. She waved her hand, but nothing happened. I pushed her onto the ground.

"Why didn't my magic work on you?" she angrily asked.

"I'm the Deliverer! You can't hurt me with your magic! Didn't you know?" I said cockily.

"But I can make things with magic and use them to hurt you," Twila said, and a sword appeared in her hand.

We both stood up. I struck at her and she blocked my cut. We both took a few swings, not fully aggressive. I needed to hit her, but I was too afraid of hurting her. Fear was something Twila did not have for other people—only for herself.

"I can spare you," Twila said, and we both stopped fighting. "We could live a wonderful life like old times. You and me... I raised you—how could you betray me with the strength I gave you? I thought I raised you better, to make the right choice and fight with me against people without magic who only cause harm. With the light rune casters, you'll have many problems—ones that your side creates! With us, you can live with pride and fight for the people with magic."

"The humans are only confused about us. They don't want to cause any harm!" I said.

"They want to experiment on you, control you, and kill you," Twila said.

"Yes, a few do," I replied. "But there are more innocent than guilty humans. Like us, there are evil and good people."

"In order to be safe, we must get rid of all of them!" she shrieked. "Don't you see? You and your family will never be safe as long as they're around!"

"No!" I said, lunging. I jumped on her and pinned her down to the ground. It was a good thing she couldn't use magic on me. "We will never be safe as long as you're around!" I took out the dagger that I had tucked in my boot a few days ago. I inched it closer and closer to her neck until I had cut off her necklace. I held the necklace in my hand. This necklace was the thing that had amplified her power. Without it she was an average Runecaster, and it was now safe in my hands.

"That's not your mission!" Twila screamed. "Kill me! I'm powerless now! Why won't you do it?"

"There's a secret tunnel. I'll give you a map and you can go," I decided. "Leave and never hurt me or anyone else ever again!" I grabbed the map out of my pocket and handed it to her. She followed me down the stairs to the tunnel. When Cameron saw us, he pulled out his sword. "Don't worry, she doesn't have any powers. She's leaving," I said.

"Open a portal," Cameron demanded.

"What?" I asked.

"I don't want her hurting anyone else, so send her to the human world," he answered.

"I don't know how," I stuttered.

"Yes, you do. I know you have it in you!" Cameron encouraged.

"I have to find the others," I said. "Stay here with her, and I'll be back as soon as I can. I'll make the portal as soon as they evacuate the tunnel."

Cameron nodded. He waved his hand, and bindings appeared around Twila. That put me at ease. Cameron would be safe, and Twila wouldn't hurt him.

I ran down the tunnel back to the fork and this time took the other path. Down this tunnel was another trapdoor. I went through, and my heart skipped a beat. There were dark rune casters' bodies lying all over the ground. Was this the cost of finding my parents? I gulped and began stepping over the bodies. Eventually, I saw five figures. I ran over to them. My parents were there. I hugged them tight.

"You're okay!" I sighed.

"Well, if you're okay, that means you defeated Twila! I couldn't be more proud of you, Emma, you truly are a hero!" my dad congratulated me.

I gulped. I wasn't going to tell them that I hadn't killed her. I mean, she couldn't hurt anyone, so what was the harm? And if I had killed her, my aunt, wouldn't I be as bad as the dark rune casters, killing a memberof my own family? I took her necklace from my pocket and handed it to my mom, but she pushed my hand away.

"No, you keep it. You earned it," my mom said.

"Did you hear about Colonel James?" Warren asked.

I nodded.

"But there are people safe now, too. Colonel James was a great man and I'm sure if he was here right now, he would be happy with the choices you made." my mom comforted.

I hadn't really had time to accept Colonel James's death. It had all come so quickly, I could only express the anger.

"Where's Cameron?" Warren asked.

I stuttered, "He's, uh…guarding the gate."

Warren gave me a strange look, knowing something was wrong.

"I have to go get him, so I'll meet you at the tunnel exit," I said. Now everyone was giving me a strange look. I exited into the tunnel before anyone could ask any questions.

Chapter 16 - Darkness Survives

"Cameron!" I yelled when I saw him. He was still guarding Twila. "We have to hurry," I said, and Cameron made the trap for Twila disappear.

I concentrated with all my might on the United States—the cities, the memories, and all the fun. A blue swirling circle appeared. I was so proud that I had done it!

"Good-bye, Twila," I said. I was actually sad, but I knew it was for the best that she left. I tried not to think about her, but rather the people I was helping by doing this. I pushed her toward the portal—but she grabbed my leg! I latched on to Cameron's hand, and Twila and I dangled in the portal.

Cameron slipped and grabbed on to the side of the portal to steady himself—but it wasn't working! "Help!" he yelled.

I heard footsteps coming down the hallway—but they weren't coming quickly enough! All I saw was my mom's and dad's faces before Cameron couldn't hold on anymore.

He, Twila, and I went hurtling through the portal.

The History of Ebonhaunt

No one knows who the first Runecasters were or how they came to exist. Mortal memory does not extend so far back. Yet legends abound – some say Runecasters are the children of demons, spawned by unholy alliances formed in exchange for secret knowledge. Some say they simply blinked into existence, fully formed and uniquely gifted. All we know is that for a time, Runecasters could only breed amongst their own kind, bound by the strictest of penalties never to mix their bloodlines with those of ordinary mortals who were not blessed with mastery of the runes. These people they called sightless.

Yet despite these precautions, Runecasters began to appear in Sightless families, offspring of Sightless parents. At first the ancient Runecaster families looked upon these newcomers with scorn. They were certain that the New Blood could never match the power of those of true Runecaster descent, no matter how numerous they became. Then a terrifying prophecy was made. This was the Prophecy of the Deliverer, telling of a New Blood who would rise to become the most powerful Runecaster the world had ever known, destined to rule for a five-hundred years.

As panic and tension spread through the Ancient Families, a new leader emerged from their ranks to assuage their fears. This was Cratus, was the son of one of the most distinguished and illustrious Runecaster houses. His lineage was impeccable, tracing all the way back to King David. He spoke with the voice of reason, offering wise counsel and sage advice. Alas, this is how the worst of tyrants so frequently begin.

Even as he urged the Ancient Families to be calm, Cratus himself grew increasingly fearful of the Prophecy, alarmed lest he should find himself deposed. As his paranoia took hold, so did his interest in the darkest of our crafts. Books began to vanish from the Athenaeum, books containing the secrets of the Forbidden Runes. Anyone who questioned Cratus' activities vanished as surely and permanently as the books.

As his knowledge and power grew, Cratus set out to recruit young members of the most ancient and prestigious families. He would charm them with his magnetic charisma, enthral them with his forbidden lore and initiate them into his personal army: The Darkcasters.

Trained as fierce warriors, the Darkcasters were deadly with blade, bow, bare hands and above all, runes. They learned the use of the Forbidden Runes under Cratus' personal instruction. He then despatched them on a series of raids, arresting every New Blood they could find and delivering them for interrogation. Threats, torture, forced confessions – Cratus would stop at nothing to discover the identity of the prophesied Deliverer. One New Blood after another died without every satisfying Cratus' demands, until finally one of them gasped a name with his dying breath. The Darkcasters swarmed upon the home of the unfortunate young man who had been named, slaying him and his entire family in a single swoop.

Ecstatic at the destruction of the supposed Deliverer, Cratus believed that nothing could harm him now. The world lay before him, his for the taking as long as his army of Darkcasters stood at his back. As proof of their loyalty and devotion to him, Cratus demanded that each of his Darkcasters sacrifice a member of his or her family. The victim would be selected at random, and the deed must be done within the fortnight by the Darkcaster's own hand.

Thus Cratus inadvertently brought about the schism that tore his army in two. Although evil lurked in the hearts of many Darkcasters, there were several who were still truly capable of love. Faced with an order that conflicted so strongly with their true natures, these young men and women could not obey. The conflict within them was so fierce that it shattered the enthralment that they had been kept under. They turned their backs on Cratus and deserted his army.

Amongst those whose enchantment had been broken was Darsaadi, Cratus' chief lieutenant. Her eyes were opened, she realised the evil she had been a part of and she was consumed with shame at the thought of what she had been. Determined to atone for her actions, she started by going to her parents to beg their forgiveness. She told them of her enthralment, her time in the Darkcaster army, of Cratus' fiendish demands, and pleaded with them not to despise her for her newfound sympathy for the New Bloods.

To her astonishment, her parents embraced her and asked her to forgive them. They told her of their younger days when they had travelled the world. They had been adventurous, eager to learn all the world had to offer, and had mixed with Runecasters and Sightless alike. Their travels took them to many places, including an impoverished town in the middle of nowhere where they sought shelter for a night in a broken down inn. There they sensed the presence of another Runecaster – the innkeeper's baby daughter. Trapped in crippling poetry, the innkeeper could scarcely afford to feed his child and feared she would not survive the coming winter. Darsaadi's parents had long grieved their lack of children, so they offered to adopt the infant and raise her as their own in all the comfort and luxury of an Ancient Family. The innkeeper gratefully accepted and was recompensed, while the baby girl was raised with love. She was never told the secret of her true origins but believed herself to be her parents' only daughter: Darsaadi.

Learning that she was truly a New Blood instilled a new resolve in Darsaadi, and she left her home filled with determination to destroy the Darkcasters. She travelled far and wide recruiting others to her cause, New Bloods, members of Ancient Families, anyone who shared her resolve to end the tyranny of the Darkcasters. She named her followers Lightcasters, boldly proclaiming the choice each Runecaster must make.

Thus began the War of Desecration, which raged for nine turbulent years, claiming thousands of lives on both sides. Darkcasters and Lightcasters alike searched for new ways to use the runes, desperately seeking the right spells bring their enemies to heel. Armed with the Forbidden Runes, the Darkcasters made a breakthrough that allowed them to spread death and disease throughout Europe. The Lightcasters' strength began to dwindle until eventually it became clear that they were facing defeat.

In an act of genius and desperation, Darsaadi surrendered to Cratus. Intending to savour his victory, he demanded she yield in person and had her brought alone and unarmed to his castle. He rejoiced to see her surrounded by his Darkcasters, clearly suffering the ravages of war. She was hunched, broken, her hands fluttering nervously, dirt ingrained in her filthy skin, muttering quietly to herself. Cratus beckoned her closer… and to his surprise, he saw a faint smile on her lips.

Too late he realised his mistake. Her skin began to glow, shining even through her clothes – the marks that Cratus had thought were dirt were in fact an intricate tattoo of complex runes, the result of weeks of painstaking work done her Lightcasters. Her fluttering hands and half-mad mumbling were really the culmination of weeks spent chanting, giving voice to the exact combination of words needed to bind the runes, activate their power and flood Darsaadi's body with the brilliant, fatal energy that now flowed from her. As she spoke her final words she exploded into golden light, surrendering her life to vanquish her enemies.

Cratus and his Darkcasters were annihilated by the blast of light, leaving nothing but their shadows which were seared into the stone walls and floor. All that remained of Cratus himself was a charred dark shape at the foot of his throne. To this day the shadows still flicker slightly, almost imperceptibly, as an unsettling reminder of the hell to which the Darkcasters were consigned.

Darsaadi lay collapsed on the floor. She had expected death, yet she was still breathing. The runes that covered her body were burned into her skin, deeper than any tattoo. In the depths of her heart she was aware of being profoundly changed. Two centuries have passed since then, yet Darsaadi has not aged a single day.

Cratus' castle became Darsaadi's stronghold. In token of our enemies' shadows being eternally seared into the stone, she named it Ebonhaunt. She set her Lightcasters two tasks: that of seeking out the remaining Darkcasters to bring them to justice, and that of destroying every shred of information regarding the use of Forbidden Runes, down to the last scrap of paper.

Darsaadi was inspired her to find ways that the Runecasters could channel the forces of nature. She created new runes that no Runecaster had ever seen before, runes designed to prevent such evil from ever holding sway again. These are the runes that have kept us hidden and protected ever since.

Darsaadi is our Deliverer.

Made in the USA
Middletown, DE
29 March 2016